MR. BUDD AGAIN

Archaeologist Reuben Hayles was under police protection after receiving a warning that his life was in imminent danger. Superintendent Budd guarded the door of his room against any intruder, with Sergeant Leek stationed outside the room's only window. Despite this, Hayles was discovered battered to death. The room was empty — devoid of any murder weapon, so the blow was not self-inflected. And a search revealed no hidden panels. How had the man been killed?

GERALD VERNER

MR. BUDD AGAIN

Complete and Unabridged

LINFORD
Leicester

First published in Great Britain

First Linford Edition
published 2012

British Library CIP Data

Verner, Gerald.
  Mr. Budd again. - - (Linford mystery library)
  1. Budd, Robert (Fictitious character)- -
  Fiction. 2. Detective and mystery stories.
  3. Large type books.
  I. Title II. Series
  823.9'12–dc23

  ISBN 978–1–4448–1043–1

Published by
F. A. Thorpe (Publishing)
Anstey, Leicestershire

Set by Words & Graphics Ltd.
Anstey, Leicestershire
Printed and bound in Great Britain by
T. J. International Ltd., Padstow, Cornwall

This book is printed on acid-free paper

To
ERNEST DUDLEY
with every good wish

THE BEARD OF
THE PROPHET

1

Mr. Budd Hears of the Prophet

That obese and sleepy-eyed detective, Superintendent Robert Budd, always referred afterwards to the queer incidents surrounding the death of old Reuben Hayles as 'that hokum business at Liddenhurst.' And to a certain extent this description was justified.

The old, neglected manor house and its strange occupant; the storm which raged throughout that terrible night, and the horrible and 'impossible' death of the old man, did not strictly belong to real life at all.

They were, as Mr. Budd remarked disparagingly at the time, 'story book stuff,' and his sense of reality was, in consequence, a little outraged.

The whole thing began on a morning in late August when he was summoned to the Assistant-Commissioner's room and found Colonel Blair, smooth and dapper as usual, examining the contents of a big folder that lay open on the desk in front of him.

'Sit down, Superintendent.' His superior nodded towards a vacant chair. 'I've got something rather queer here. You've heard of Reuben Hayles, I suppose?'

'The archaeologist feller?' murmured the big man, and the Assistant-Commissioner inclined his head.

'That's the man,' he said. 'The newspapers were full of him six months ago. He was supposed to have discovered the tomb of Mohammed. There was great excitement at the time. Professor This said he had, and Professor That said he hadn't. Letters were written to *The Times* praising him and abusing him alternately. He read a paper to the Archaeological Society, proving conclusively that he had found the tomb of the prophet, and another distinguished gentleman read a paper proving equally conclusively that he'd done nothing of the kind. Nobody, apparently, has the least idea which is right.'

The fat man blinked sleepily. Certainly he hadn't, and he didn't very much care.

'Well, it appears,' continued Colonel Blair, 'that this man Hayles has recently been receiving a series of threatening letters. Instead of disregarding them, as the majority of people would, he seems to have taken a serious view. So much so, in fact, that he has asked for police investigation and protection.'

'Surely, sir,' murmured Mr. Budd, raising his eyebrows in surprise, 'it's a matter for the local police to deal with?'

'In the ordinary course, yes,' said his superior. 'But Hayles is a distant cousin of the Home Secretary, and he has particularly requested that we should look into the matter. Liddenhurst, where Hayles lives, is on the edge of the Metropolitan area, so I'm sending you down to pacify the old man.

'It's unusual, I know,' went on the Assistant-Commissioner, when he saw Mr. Budd's expression, 'to detail such a trivial case to any officer of your rank — but the circumstances are exceptional. Personally I don't suppose for one minute that there's anything in these threats. They're the usual sort of twaddle, but there you are.' He shrugged his shoulders and flicked open the folder in front of him. 'Here are the letters,' he said, pushing the cardboard cover across the desk, and Mr. Budd sat forward wearily, and inspected the contents.

They consisted of four sheets of cheap notepaper and the messages, which had been typewritten, were short. The first was dated July 15th, and ran:

'Your sacrilege will bring violent death in its train. Take heed for your time is short.'

It was signed: 'The Prophet.'
And the second, which was dated ten days later read:

'Every passing hour brings your doom nearer. The curse is upon you.'

The date of the third was only a week after the second:

'I am coming for you soon. The hand of Mohammed is raised to strike.'

There was an interval between this and the last of nearly three weeks, and the threat became more definite.

'Death will come to you on the night of the full moon. Prepare to meet your doom.'

Mr. Budd sniffed disparagingly when he had read the last of the notes.

'The Prophet!' he muttered contemptuously. 'Some crazy fanatic, I suppose. I can't understand any sane man taking this nonsense seriously, sir.'

'Neither can I,' said Colonel Blair, 'but there it is. Hayles may be eccentric, but he's certainly not mad, and he evidently takes these threats very seriously indeed. Tomorrow night is the night of the full moon,' he added.

'And Mr. Hayles, bein' scared, wants somebody there in case this prophet feller turns up as promised,' murmured the stout man.

'Exactly!' The Assistant-Commissioner helped himself to a cigarette, lit it, and nodded through the smoke.

'When d'you suggest I go, sir?' asked Mr. Budd, without enthusiasm.

'Tomorrow morning,' answered Blair. 'In the meanwhile, you'd better take these letters and see if you can learn anything.'

The stout superintendent picked up the folder and tucked it under his arm.

'I'll take Sergeant Leek with me, sir,' he said, pausing at the door. 'I don't suppose anythin' 'ull happen, but just in case it does we'd better do the thing according to routine.'

He left London at ten o'clock on the following morning in his dingy little car, accompanied by the lean sergeant, and neither experienced any premonition of the tragedy that was awaiting them.

It was a hot, still morning; there was not a breath of air and the atmosphere was stifling. Neither was it appreciably cooler when they reached the open country. The sun beat down from a cloudless sky, and the surrounding countryside lay parched and scorching beneath its glare.

Liddenhurst was a tiny village with a handful of houses and a whitewashed inn. The road to the Manor House wound through dips and hollows overhung by trees, for the welcome shade of which Mr. Budd was grateful. They passed a small, square-towered, church of great age with tombstones clustering closely round it, and turned into the right hand branch of a fork. A mile farther on they came in sight of the entrance to the drive, and it was not prepossessing. The lodge was a ruin; the gates decayed structures of rotting timber.

The stout man slowed the car and eyed the faded inscription on the crumbling pillars.

'This is the place,' he said, and Leek glanced dubiously at the weed-grown approach, twisting between unkempt shrubs.

'Don't look as if anybody's been here for years,' he remarked, and the stout superintendent agreed.

But there was the name — readable, if only just — and he swung the car into the

9

drive. Rounding the bend he saw before him a big, rambling house, ivy covered, and set amid a profusion of rank grass, weeds, and nettles. A great cedar tree grew in front of the porch, and in spite of the brightness of the sun its black, plate-like branches gave a sinister aspect to the place.

Mr. Budd thought it was not surprising that a man living in such a house should be troubled with nervous fancies. He began to feel a little dispirited himself.

He brought the car to a halt and got laboriously down in front of an ivy-covered porch, mounted the shallow, moss-stained steps, and pulled at a rusty iron bell. After some delay the door was opened by a thin man with a tremendous nose, who peered at him shortsightedly.

'Mr. Hayles live here?' murmured the fat detective.

'Yes, sir,' said the owner of the nose. Its use was now obvious, for he talked through it. 'Are you the gentleman he's expecting?'

'I'm from Scotland Yard,' grunted the superintendent, and produced a card.

The large-nosed man invited him into the hall.

'If you'll wait just a moment, sir,' he said nasally, 'I'll tell Mr. Hayles you're here.'

He took the card and hurried away up the wide staircase. The interior of the house was in keeping with the outside. The big entrance hall was gloomy; the panelling dull and lifeless; the parquet floor worn. The musty odour, which is usually associated with houses that have long been shut up, filled the air, and even the copper bowl of sickly-looking flowers that stood upon an old gate-legged table, failed to dispel the dreariness.

Mr. Budd looked about him and mopped his perspiring forehead, wondering whether Mr. Hayles kept any beer in the house. There was a faint murmur of voices emanating from somewhere, and he had just located it as coming from behind a closed door on the right, when the servant appeared halfway down the staircase and called to him. With Leek at his heels the big man mounted the broad stairs, was conducted along a corridor,

11

and ushered into the presence of Mr. Reuben Hayles.

The archaeologist was sitting at an enormous desk, which was littered with books and papers; an elderly, bald-headed, whiskered man, with large horn-rimmed glasses and a grey, stubbly chin.

'Sit down, Superintendent. Sit down,' he said in a high-pitched, querulous voice. 'I'm very glad to see you.'

Mr. Budd sat down.

'This is Sergeant Leek, sir,' he murmured. 'I thought it best to bring him with me.'

The man behind the desk nodded. He was palpably nervous. His face twitched spasmodically, and his thin hands kept moving restlessly, touching the various objects within his reach on the desk with jerky movements.

'I've seen the letters which were sent to you,' said Mr. Budd, breaking a rather awkward silence. 'And I understand that you attach importance to them?'

'Do not you?' asked the old man quickly.

'To be quite candid, I don't, sir,'

answered the Superintendent, shaking his head. 'I've seen too many such things in my time to take 'em seriously. There's a class of person who can't help writin' anonymous letters. It's a kink. It's my belief that you're just a victim of one of these queer people. That is, of course, unless you have anythin' more tangible to go on.'

'No, no, I haven't!' the archaeologist broke in quickly. 'I must admit, however, that these — er — communications have disturbed me, particularly in view of my recent discovery of Mohammed's tomb. Whether anything occurs tonight or not, I'm greatly relieved to have you, and — er — the sergeant on the premises. Greatly relieved!'

There was fear in the faded eyes, and Mr. Budd received the impression that Reuben Hayles knew a lot more than he had said. It was inconceivable that a man of his intelligence should have been reduced to such a state of mind merely by the receipt of those childish letters. There was something else, something more practical that had brought that lurking fear to his eyes and induced him to apply for police protection. His thoughts were interrupted by a tap on the door and somebody came in.

'Oh, it's you, Brown!' The old man looked up over Mr. Budd's head. 'Er — Superintendent. Meet my secretary, Mr. Washington Brown.'

Mr. Budd turned to greet the newcomer, and suppressed a gasp of surprise.

2

The People of the Manor House

Washington Brown bowed, smiling pleasantly and revealing in the process a remarkably perfect set of milk-white teeth, contrasting sharply with his coal-black skin.

'I must apologise for interrupting your conference, sir,' he said in faultless English. 'I was unaware you had anyone with you. I have only just returned from the post office with the stamps.' He came over to the desk and placed a stamp book in front of his employer.

'Thank you, Brown,' murmured the archaeologist. 'You didn't interrupt us. There's nothing secret about the reason for these — er — gentlemen being here.' He glanced at a softly ticking clock in front of him. 'Luncheon will be ready in twenty minutes, and I've no doubt they would like a wash after their journey. Will you find Murley and have them shown to their rooms?'

'Certainly, sir.' The secretary went over to the door and opened it. 'Will you come with me, please, gentlemen?'

Mr. Budd extricated himself from the rather close embrace of the chair in which he had been sitting, and stood up.

'Please make yourselves quite at home,' said the old man. 'I am extremely busy at the moment on my new book. If there's anything you want, ask Brown or Murley and they will attend to it. I will see you at luncheon.' He picked up a pen and bent over his work, and they followed the secretary out into the corridor.

Closing the door softly behind him, Washington Brown murmured a polite excuse, went to the head of the stairs and called. After a short delay, the big-nosed man appeared. He listened a little sullenly to Brown's orders, and then, when the secretary, with a smile of startling brilliancy, left them, proceeded to carry out his instructions.

The rooms that had been allotted to them were on the floor above, and commanded a view of the neglected parkland. They were large and rather drab, hung with faded chintz, and sparsely furnished. Murley pointed out a bathroom at the end of the corridor showed them where their bags had been put, inquired if there was anything else they wanted, and took his departure.

Leek lingered in Mr. Budd's room, a lugubrious expression on his lean face.

'Rum sort of place, ain't it?' he remarked,

The stout man grunted as he unpacked his bag. Some of the archaeologist's obvious uneasiness seemed to have communicated itself to him, or perhaps it was the atmosphere that pervaded the whole house that made him feel vaguely conscious of a sense of impending trouble. Was there really some potent danger surrounding Reuben Hayles? Or was it only the old man's imagination?

Looked at in the setting of that dilapidated mansion with its musty smelling, disused, atmosphere and unkempt grounds, the business of the anonymous threats took on a more sinister aspect. He began to wonder if anything would happen after all that night, the night on which the moon reached its full.

It was difficult to be sceptical with the memory of that fear which he had seen shining nakedly from the old man's eyes. He, at least, believed in the prophet's prophecy.

He went into the bathroom for a wash, trying vainly to shake off his sudden depression. But it remained, an unpleasant feeling which refused to yield to sane thinking.

A brazen gong echoed through the house to signal the serving of lunch, and Mr. Budd, followed by the rather self-conscious and nervous Leek, went down. He was met in the hall by Murley, and conducted to the dining room.

It was a long, low-raftered room, with french windows, opening on to what had, at one time, been a lawn, but which was now nothing more than a waist-high tangle of weeds and rank grass. At the long table that occupied the centre of the room, seven people were seated. The butler ushered the big superintendent and the sergeant into the two vacant chairs, and Mr. Hayles at the head of the table, introduced them to his household.

They were a queer lot of people. There was a small man of unhealthy-looking fatness, with a thick moustache and large, surprised eyes as though he lived in a constant state of astonishment at everything that was going on around him. His name Mr. Budd did not quite catch, but it sounded like Glibber. He was a cousin of Hayles', and apparently also interested in archaeology. The superintendent thought this may have accounted for his having married Mrs. Glibber, a thin, gaunt woman, with a long dark face and hollow eyes, whose age might have been anything between fifty and a hundred and twenty, so dried up and lifeless did she appear.

Next to this unpleasant-looking female was a young man with watery eyes, a pimple of a chin, and rather long, lank, fair hair, that fell over his forehead every time he moved his head, and which he had a nervous habit of brushing back as though he was being bothered with flies. His name was Dinwater, and he was, apparently, their host's nephew.

On the right of the old man was a curious-looking, olive-skinned man of foreign appearance, with deep, brown, dog-like eyes, whose nationality was evidently Turkish, for he was introduced to Mr. Budd as Mahmoud Bey. And, lastly, there was the girl.

Kathleen Travers was slight and fair, and if she was not the type that a magazine artist would have used as a model for a cover design, she was pretty in a pale, rather washed-out way. She also, the stout man discovered later, was a relation.

They all eyed Mr. Budd and the lean sergeant covertly and curiously. Apparently the reason for their presence was general knowledge, for the subject of the prophet letters was brought up almost immediately and discussed at length by everybody with the exception of the girl and Washington Brown, who listened in silence.

What surprised the detective most was that they all seemed to regard the matter as serious, although nobody seemed to have the slightest inkling concerning the identity of the writer. There was also another thing which Mr. Budd's sleepy-looking eyes detected, and that was a veiled antagonism between them. They watched each other with a kind of suspicious alertness, as though each was afraid of what the other might say next.

Altogether a queer lot, the big man decided.

Sergeant Leek, embarrassed and confused by the unusual array of spoons and knives and forks beside his plate, sat in gloomy silence, eating whatever was set before him, and praying inwardly that the meal would shortly come to an end.

It did eventually, and he and Mr. Budd escaped into weed-grown garden.

'Funny bunch, ain't they?' said Leek, shaking his head mournfully. 'That girl was all right, though.'

'Now don't you go gettin' sentimental,' warned Mr. Budd severely.

'What d'you mean?' protested the sergeant indignantly. 'I was only contrasting her with the rest of 'em.'

Mr. Budd grunted, and wiped his damp face. The heat was stifling, a humid, airless heat which induced a feeling of limpness. There was a haze in the sky and a tinge of copper, which he surveyed critically.

'Shouldn't be surprised if we were in for a storm,' he murmured. 'I should think that's what it was working up for.'

'I 'ope not,' said Leek anxiously. 'Storms always make me feel queer.'

'You're always queer!' growled Mr. Budd. 'You was born queer. You must have been the queerest baby in the world!'

'I was considered a fine child — ' began the sergeant.

'By the Zoological Society, I suppose,' broke in the superintendent rudely, and Leek tried vainly to think of a suitable retort for this insulting remark. 'Pity to let a fine place like this go to rack and ruin,' went on the big man. 'This must have been a garden worth seein' at one time.'

They had come to the end of a bramble-lined path, which led to a ramshackle summerhouse, and, turning, he eyed the old, ivy-covered building, with its quaint gables and leaded windows, a little sorrowfully, wondering why old Reuben Hayles had allowed his property to fall into such a dilapidated state.

Close to the house grew an ancient oak tree of gigantic stature, its gnarled branches almost touching the walls in some places — a majestic tree, in keeping with its surroundings.

The rest of the day passed slowly. Tea was served in an old-fashioned drawing room, but Mr. Hayles was not present. He was working, the secretary announced, and did not wish to be disturbed.

After dinner, at which the old man looked even more nervous than he had done in the morning, he had a brief interview with Mr. Budd, in the hall.

'You will make your own arrangements, Superintendent,' he said, glancing quickly about him. 'I shall probably be working until fairly late with my secretary.'

'I'm proposin',' said the stout man, 'to put Sergeant Leek on guard outside the house, and look after the inside meself.'

'I sincerely hope,' muttered the archae-ologist, passing the tip of his tongue across his lips, 'that the precautions will be unnecessary.'

'I hope so too, sir,' said Mr. Budd, and watched him curiously as he made his way uncertainly up the big staircase.

The sun had set in an angry bank of purple and red cloud, and when it disappeared a strange stillness settled over the countryside. Not a single leaf stirred, and there was a deep hush, as though every living thing had suddenly held its breath.

Mr. Budd got hold of Murley, and from that unprepossessing man obtained a very good idea of the layout of the house. He drew a rough plan on a page of his notebook, so that he could find his way about easily, scribbling the names of the people who occupied the various bedrooms in their appropriate places.

Reuben Hayles slept in a room adjoining his study, and on the same floor were Professor Glibber and his wife, and Kathleen Travers. On the floor above were five bedrooms occupied respectively by Leek, Mr. Budd himself, Geoffrey Dinwater, Mahmoud Bey, and the secretary.

The servants' quarters were shut off from the rest of the house by a door to which Murley alone had a key. This door was locked at night and opened in the morning, together with another door on the ground floor, which cut off the kitchen and the entire back premises.

Having primed himself with these details, Mr. Budd made a slow and ponderous round of the rooms on the ground floor, examining the window fastenings. In contrast to the rest of the house they were new and recently fitted. It would be a clever person who could force those patent catches.

When he had completed his survey, he went in search of Leek. He found the sergeant in his room reading an evening paper, which he had borrowed from one of the servants.

'It's time you began to earn your salary,' he said, glancing at his watch. 'You know what you've got to do? Patrol the side of the house under Mr. Hayles' study. That'll ensure that no one can come any funny tricks that way. You understand?'

The sergeant nodded.

'What are you goin' to do?' he asked.

'I'm goin' to sit in a comfortable chair,' said his superior, 'in the corridor on which the study and the bedroom doors open, so that nobody can get at the old man from that direction.'

Leek sighed.

'You always choose the best jobs,' he grumbled. 'Why can't I do that — '

'Because I've told you to do somethin' else!' retorted Mr. Budd. 'What's the use of reachin' the rank of superintendent if you can't pick the cushy jobs!'

As this was unanswerable, Leek said nothing

'Now you get along,' said the big man. 'If there's any disturbance, blow your whistle.'

The melancholy sergeant rose gloomily to his feet. 'I expect it'll all be a waste of time,' he muttered. 'So far as I can see, we might just as well be comfortable in our beds.'

'We've come here to guard the old man,' declared Mr. Budd, 'and whether anythin' happens or not we're goin' to do it! Now get along and don't argue!'

The sergeant 'got along', and the superintendent tucking the newspaper under his arm, went to seek the chair that he had ordered Murley to place into position for him. He found it set against the wall in the corridor, and within sight of the study door. The light that hung from the ceiling was dim, but it was sufficient to enable him to see, and he settled himself comfortably.

The drone of a voice reached his ears from behind the closed door of the room in which Mr. Hayles was working, and he concluded that the archaeologist was dictating to his secretary.

At eleven o'clock the other members of the household began to retire for the night. Professor Glibber and his wife were the first to seek their rooms. They came along the corridor, stared curiously at the watchful Mr. Budd, muttered a curt 'good night', and disappeared through a door at the other end of the passage. After an interval, Mahmoud Bey came slowly up the stairs. He stopped at the end of the corridor, glanced along it, and continued up the second flight to the floor above. At a quarter to twelve Kathleen Travers and Geoffrey Dinwater came up the stairs together. They paused on the landing, stood talking for a moment or two, and then the girl said 'good night', and came rapidly along the passage. She gave a startled gasp as she saw Mr. Budd, and stopped.

'Oh!' she stammered. 'You — you frightened me for a moment. Are you stopping here all night?'

'Most of it, I expect, miss,' he answered.

'I — I hope nothing happens,' she said, and he smiled.

'I don't think it will,' he replied reassuringly. 'I don't see very well how it can.'

She wished him 'good night', and went into her room.

The voice behind the study door was still murmuring monotonously. Presently Mr. Budd heard the sound of Murley locking up, and shortly after the butler appeared.

'I've locked and bolted all the doors

and fastened the windows, sir,' he said. 'Is there anything further you require?'

The stout man shook his head.

'No, thank you,' he answered.

'Then I'll wish you 'good night', sir,' answered the butler, and went down the big staircase.

The light in the hall went out, followed by the sound of the closing and locking of the communicating door to the back premises. Mr. Budd settled himself more comfortably, took out one of his thin black cigars, and eyed it regretfully. He would have liked to smoke, but the odour would percolate to the bedrooms and possibly annoy the occupants. He put it away with a sigh, and as he did so a low rumble of thunder came to his ears. A flicker of lightning lit up the landing eerily. The storm he had predicted earlier had burst.

3

Night of the Full Moon

For many months afterwards Mr. Budd referred to that night at the old manor house as the first time he had ever seriously believed in the supernatural. For what eventually happened, was, by all the laws of nature, impossible.

It was one o'clock when the door of the study opened and the secretary appeared on the threshold.

'Good night, sir,' he called softly as he came out, closing the door behind him.

'Mr. Hayles all right?' murmured Mr. Budd as the man came level with him.

Washington Brown nodded.

'Perfectly all right, sir,' he answered, with a great display of teeth. 'He's just going to bed.' He wished the stout superintendent 'good night' and passed on his way.

The rumble of thunder was almost

continuous and getting louder. The storm was drawing nearer. Mr. Budd thought of Leek keeping his vigil in the open, and hoped he had had the forethought to provide himself with a coat. He would need it before the night was through.

A quarter of an hour went by after the passing of the secretary, and then once again the study door opened and the old man came out into the corridor. He peered in the direction of Mr. Budd, switched out the light, shut the door, and came over to him.

'I'm going to bed now, Superintendent,' he said wearily. 'I trust there will be no disturbance.'

'I don't think you need worry, sir,' said Mr. Budd. 'You can sleep quite happily. I shall be here for the rest of the night, and Sergeant Leek is outside your window. It's impossible for anyone to get near you without passin' one or other of us.'

'The arrangement seems very satisfactory.' The archaeologist nodded. 'Good night — er — Superintendent. If there's anything you require, don't hesitate to wake Murley.'

He nodded again, went over to the door adjoining that of the study, opened it, and disappeared within.

Mr. Budd yawned. He was not tired, but his vigil was a little boring. It was unlikely that anything would happen. His premonition had been the outcome of the house and its surroundings. Possibly the gathering storm, too, had played its part in producing that vague uneasiness that had grown on him throughout the day. Nothing could happen to old Hayles. The letters were just a lot of nonsense, the crazy threat of some weak-minded, religious fanatic! It was queer, though —

He was on his feet instantly as the sound reached him; a smothered exclamation, a thin scream, and the thud of a falling body. It came from the door of the room through which a moment before the archaeologist had disappeared.

In two strides Mr. Budd had reached the portal.

'Is anythin' the matter, sir?' he called, but there was no reply.

Twisting the handle he flung open the door and entered. A deafening crash of thunder came rolling in through the open windows simultaneously with a vivid blue-white glare. It lit the room weirdly, putting to shame the shaded lamp, and revealing with startling clearness the sprawling figure that lay on the floor. It was Reuben Hayles!

There was blood on his face and spattered on the floor around him. The front of his head was crushed in, the result of a terrible blow that must have killed him instantly. He lay in the centre of the apartment on an ancient rug.

Mr. Budd stared at him incredulously. Apart from himself and the crumpled figure the room was empty.

Swiftly he closed the door, turned the key, and went over to the window. Another flash of violent white light split the sky and a rolling boom of thunder went reverberating over the house as he leaned out and called to Leek. The thin sergeant appeared instantly.

'Did anyone come out of this window?' snapped Mr. Budd.

'Come out of this window?' repeated the bewildered Leek. 'No. Nobody ain't come out nor gone in. Why? What's 'appened?'

'Hayles has been murdered!' snarled the superintendent, but his words were drowned in another peal of thunder. 'Stay where you are!' He withdrew his head as big drops of rain began to fall rapidly, went over to the body and, kneeling down, felt for the heart. There was no movement.

The old man was dead. There was no doubt of that. But how he had met his death was a mystery of mysteries,

The big man made a rapid search of the room. There was nobody concealed under the bed or in the large wardrobe, nor any sign of the weapon that must have been used to inflict such a terrible wound.

Mr. Budd rubbed his massive chin and stared about him blankly. The blow had been struck with tremendous force, and even if someone had concealed himself in the room earlier in the evening and waited for the old man to enter, it was impossible for him to have escaped. He himself had been within sight of the door all the time, and Leek was below the window. No one could have got out of that room.

He felt a little chill in the region of his spine. There was no natural explanation. What was it that had come out of the stormy night, killed, and vanished again, leaving no trace of its passage?

He shook off the superstitious fear that had momentarily taken possession of him. This was murder, and there was plenty to do. This was no time for fancies and imaginings. He made another search of the room, the vague possibility of some secret entrance crossing his mind. It was an old house, and such things were not unknown.

But he found nothing of the kind. The floor was solid, the walls, too. There was no place for a dog to have lain concealed, let alone a human being. Yet there on the floor at his feet lay the shattered body of a man who had been killed by a savage blow; a blow that had been dealt by a powerful hand.

He went over to the window once more.

'You there, Leek?' he called. 'I want you up here right away. Can you get in?'

Leek looked up pathetically through the drenching rain.

'Not unless someone lets me in,' he answered.

'Well, ring the bell,' said Mr. Budd. 'And keep ringing till you wake the servants.'

The lightning came again as the sergeant slouched away, and a thunderous detonation shook the house. Mr. Budd stared at the oak tree silhouetted against the glare, and wondered if it was possible for anyone to have swung from the window into the branches. He shook his head. It was too far away, and, anyhow, the accompanying noise would have been heard by Leek, unless — a thought occurred to him — unless the thunder had drowned it!

He wondered if he had discovered the explanation, but after a moment's consideration he saw that it was practically impossible. No man could have carried out such a feat in the time.

The muffled pealing of the bell reached

his ears as he turned back to the room. How long would Leek be before he was successful in rousing the house? Nobody as yet appeared to be aware that anything out of the ordinary had happened, or if they were they had given no sign,

He looked down at the dead man, and his face was stern. He felt, to a certain extent, responsible. The old man had asked him for protection, and he had failed him. Yet he could have done no more than he had. He had taken what he considered were adequate precautions. They should have been adequate. A guard on the window, a guard on the door. It was impossible for anyone to have reached the man. And yet here was proof positive that somebody had.

He took out his handkerchief and wiped his perspiring face, and his usual sleepy expression had vanished completely.

The pealing of the bell went on monotonously. Somebody must hear it sooner or later. The local police would have to be notified, a doctor sent for, and then he saw something he had not noticed before.

The old man had fallen on his back, arms flung wide. And in one of his hands was something dark. He bent down and peered at the object, gently moved the body to get a better view, and stared in open-mouthed astonishment, for the thing which Reuben Hayles held clenched in his dead fingers was a beard of dark grey hair. And it was a false beard! The wire frame to which the hair was attached was plainly visible.

Mr. Budd straightened up, went over to the bed and sat down. His thoughts were chaotic, and he found it difficult to think clearly. A phrase that he had heard kept repeating itself over and over again: 'The beard of the prophet. The beard of the prophet. The beard of the prophet.' He had read it in books, heard it on the films. It was a commonplace oath of the East. 'By the beard of the prophet.' And it was the Prophet who had sent the threatening letters; the Prophet who had carried out his threat and left, leaving his beard behind.

It was insane! A nightmare! But it was true!

Mr. Budd passed a hand over his eyes wearily, almost as though he expected to find that he was dreaming. But it was no dream. There was old Reuben Hayles — dead. There in his hand was a grey beard. And here was Mr. Budd prepared to swear before any jury that nobody could have entered or left the room in which he had been killed.

The pealing of the bell stopped abruptly, and he heard voices. Presently there was a step in the corridor outside, and getting up, he walked to the door, turned the key, and opened it. Murley, a grotesque figure in a tattered dressing gown, his eyes heavy with sleep, was standing on the threshold with Leek by his side.

'What's happened?' he whispered. 'What's happened?'

'Your master's been killed!' said Mr. Budd shortly. 'Is there a telephone in the house?'

'Yes, sir, in the study,' answered the butler, trying to catch a glimpse of the bedroom beyond the figure of the stout man. 'But — but how did — '

'I've no time to answer questions!' snapped Mr. Budd brusquely. 'Telephone the nearest police station. Ask for the divisional inspector. Say that murder has been committed, and will he come here as soon as possible.'

'Murder!' Murley gasped the word. 'Mr. Hayles — Mr. Hayles has been murdered?'

'Yes!' snarled Mr. Budd. 'Go and do as I tell you!'

The butler opened his mouth, closed it again, and hurried away. Leek, with dropped jaw and wide eyes, was staring at his superior.

'You don't mean — the old man's been killed?' he whispered incredulously.

'Didn't you hear what I told you from the window, or don't I speak plainly enough?' said Mr. Budd irritably, 'If I said he was murdered he must have been killed!'

'But — how — when?' stammered the sergeant incoherently.

'He was killed in this room less than a quarter of an hour ago,' said Mr. Budd impressively. 'He was killed while you were under the window and I was outside the door! And the murderer's escaped. Now work that out!'

'But — but it's impossible,' blurted Leek. 'I'll swear nobody got away by the window.'

'And I'll swear nobody got away by the door,' growled the big man. 'But Hayles is dead from a blow on the head. There's no weapon, and he's clutching a false beard in his hand. If you can explain that you're cleverer than I am!'

The sergeant moved forward so that he could get a view of the interior of the room, and gasped.

'Don't stand gapin' there!' said his superior. 'Go along and wake the rest of the household. Explain what's happened, and take 'em down to the drawing room. Hold 'em there till I've got time to see 'em.'

'But how could it have happened?' muttered the dazed Leek. 'It's not possible — '

'Don't start an argument!' snarled Mr. Budd. 'Just do as I tell you for once without talkin'. The only thing I can think of is that there must be some other exit from this room which we've yet to discover. Now, go along and wake those people.'

The sergeant departed, and Mr. Budd once more closed and locked the door. Pulling a chair from the wall he sat down and tried to concentrate his thoughts on the problem that had been presented to him. And it was the biggest one he had ever come up against.

Somebody had got into the room and somebody had got out, and they hadn't come either by the door or the window. So there must be another way in. In that case the mystery was less difficult. But if there was such a thing it was very cleverly concealed. He had found no trace of it, but that didn't say it wasn't there. He realised with something of a shock that that was the first thing that had to be proved — how it was possible for the crime to have been committed. After that it would be time to seek for the murderer. But even if they were aware who had killed the old man the knowledge would be useless until it could be logically shown how the person had entered and left the room, the window and the door of which had been under observation at the time. No jury would convict unless that could be shown.

He heard the sound of knocking, the whispering of voices, the low cry of a woman, and guessed that Leek was carrying out instructions. Presently stumbling footsteps passed the door and faded to silence. There was a tap, and he demanded to know who was there. Murley's voice answered:

'The police are on their way, sir,' said the butler. 'Is there anything else I can do?'

'Wake the servants,' said Mr. Budd curtly. 'We shall need to question them, too.'

The man went away, and the superintendent returned to his troubled thoughts. The thunder and lightning were incessant; the rain was falling in sheets. It was, he thought grimly, a fitting accompaniment for the tragedy that had taken place under his very nose.

That's what rankled. He had come to

guard this man against injury, and he had failed. There would be a severe reprimand, apart from any personal feelings he might have in the matter.

His gloomy musings were interrupted presently by the sound of a car coming up the drive, and he roused himself wearily. There was work to be done; the local police had arrived.

4

The Impossible Crime

The divisional inspector was a florid-faced, youngish-looking man, with a soft voice that seemed curiously out of place in a policeman. He was accompanied by a portly little man whom he introduced to Mr. Budd as Dr. Scavage.

'This seems to be an extraordinary business, sir,' he said in hushed tones, looking down at the body after Mr. Budd had briefly explained the circumstances. 'Sounds impossible to me.'

'Sounds impossible to me, too!' declared the big man. 'And it is impossible, the way I've described it. And yet, that's how it happened.'

'Could the murderer have been hiding and slipped out while your attention was distracted?' asked Divisional Inspector Hadlow.

Mr. Budd shook his head.

'No,' he answered. 'He had no opportunity. From the moment I made the discovery until now I've been careful not to leave the room for a moment. There's only one sensible explanation, and that is that there's a concealed entrance somewhere.'

The portly doctor, who had been making a brief examination, rose to his feet.

'He must have died instantly,' he said. 'I doubt if he knew what killed him.'

'Can you suggest what did kill him?' asked the superintendent.

Scavage pursed his lips.

'It's a little difficult,' he answered. 'It was something heavy and blunt, and a great amount of force must have been used. You found no weapon in the room?'

'No,' said Mr. Budd. 'There was no weapon and no killer, only a body.'

'But that's ridiculous!' suggested the doctor. 'It's impossible for Hayles to have struck the blow himself, and even if he did he couldn't have got rid of the weapon.'

'It is ridiculous,' murmured Mr. Budd. He had recovered from his first shock and was rapidly becoming more like his normal self. 'It is ridiculous, and there-fore it's all wrong.'

'What d'you mean?' asked the police surgeon.

'I mean,' explained the stout man carefully, 'that if it sounds impossible and ridiculous as it happened, then it didn't happen like that at all.'

'But,' said the puzzled doctor, 'you've just told us that it did.'

'I've just told you how it appeared to have happened,' answered the big man. 'There's no doubt that poor feller was murdered, or that he died from a violent blow on the head which crushed his skull. Or that he died with a false beard in his hand without anybody bein' in the room at the time. Now that's ridiculous! That's impossible! Therefore there must have been somebody in the room. But they didn't go out through the door, and they didn't go out through the window. Therefore they must have gone out somewhere else. I know that sounds a little silly, but it's logic.'

'The chimney,' put in Hadlow. 'Have you — '

'I've examined the chimney,' broke in Mr. Budd. 'It's big enough, but it's got bars across. Nobody could have got in or out that way.'

Dr. Scavage made an impatient gesture.

'The only thing I can suggest,' he said, 'is that the person must have concealed himself behind the door, waited until you'd entered the room, and then slipped out.'

'And that he couldn't have done,' declared Mr. Budd, 'because when I opened the door I kept the handle in my hand. There was no chance of anyone slippin' by without my seein' them.'

'Then there's only one explanation left,' said the doctor with conviction. 'There must be another entrance.'

Hadlow had brought a sergeant and constable with him. The sergeant was called up. Mr. Budd, the divisional inspector, and this man made a meticulous search of every inch of the apartment, but no trace or sign of any secret door or an opening in the walls or ceiling could they discover. No possible way by which the killer could have entered or left the room. The house was well built, the walls were eighteen inches thick, and the whole room was as solid as a bank vault. The door and window offered the only way of exit or entrance. Yet the murderer could have used neither. His coming and going was an impenetrable mystery.

'Well, that's that!' said Mr. Budd wearily. 'We've established one thing, anyway.'

'We've established an impossibility, sir,' pointed out Hadlow.

Dr. Scavage, who had been watching with interest, uttered an exclamation.

'Look here,' he said suddenly, 'the window was open, wasn't it, when you made the discovery?'

'It was,' admitted the big man.

'Well, couldn't something have been catapulted or thrown from outside?'

It was Hadlow who shook his head.

'If that had been the case, doctor,' he said, 'the thing would be here.'

'Yes, that's true,' said Scavage disappointedly.

'Apart from which,' remarked Mr. Budd, 'it would have taken some force to have thrown anything large enough to have inflicted that wound. No, I don't think that's how it was done.'

He walked thoughtfully over to the window and looked out. The storm was still raging. At intermittent intervals the park and the surrounding country were lit up by the lightning, and the rolling peals of thunder followed one another in quick succession.

'I'm wondering,' he said, 'if that tree could have had anything to do with it?'

Hadlow was an intelligent man and grasped his meaning quickly.

'You mean could the murderer have reached the window from the tree and got back the same way?' he said.

Mr. Budd nodded.

'I don't see how,' said the divisional inspector. 'It's a good fifteen feet away. I don't see how anyone could have bridged the gap.'

'Well, then, I give it up,' murmured Mr. Budd despairingly. 'This 'ull go down on records as the first crime to have been committed by an invisible man. An invisible man wearin' a false beard,' he added. 'It's insane!'

5

Mr. Budd Meets the Prophet

The body of the dead man was covered with a sheet but otherwise left exactly as it had been found. It could not be moved until after the police photographs had been taken, and this would have to wait until the morning. The window was closed and latched and the door locked, and when Mr. Budd had put the key in his pocket he went down, accompanied by the divisional inspector, to interview the people of the household, leaving the local sergeant on guard in the corridor.

The storm was still raging with unabated fury. The rain hissed and splashed and the thunder roared and boomed, filling the night with a deafening clamour.

Murley was in the hall talking to a stolid-looking constable when they reached the foot of the stairs, and he came over as soon as he saw the big man.

'The servants are all up, sir,' he said in a low voice. 'They're all in the kitchen, if you want to see them.'

'I'll see 'em presently,' said Mr. Budd, and went over to the door of the drawing room.

There was no sound from within, and turning the handle he entered. The six occupants were grouped in uneasy silence round the fireplace, and Leek, who was sitting uncomfortably on the edge of a chair near the door, looked up with relief when they came in. Mr. Budd paused for a moment on the threshold, sleepily eyeing the sketchily attired assemblage, before he shut the door behind him and advanced further into the room.

It was Geoffrey Dinwater who was the first to speak.

'Is it true — about Uncle Reuben?' he demanded, blinking nervously.

'I'm afraid it is, sir,' answered the stout superintendent. 'Mr. Hayles is dead!'

A variety of expressions crossed the staring faces before him, a whole gamut of emotions ranging from fear to incredulity.

'How — ' The secretary began the question and stopped.

'He was murdered,' said Mr. Budd bluntly.

Kathleen Travers caught her breath with a queer, gasping sound, and her face went white to the lips. Mahmoud Bey remained silent, but his eyes fastened themselves on Mr. Budd in an unwavering and rather disconcerting stare. Glibber clicked his teeth, and his habitually astonished face was so ludicrous that the big man felt an almost uncontrollable desire to laugh. Mrs. Glibber stared at the empty grate, her face devoid of any emotion whatever. The girl cleared her throat huskily.

'I — I can't believe it,' she muttered unsteadily. 'How did it happen? Who killed him?'

'That's what I'd like to know, miss,' said the fat detective. 'I'd very much like to know who killed him — and how!'

'How?' Glibber repeated the word in a questioning tone. 'D'you mean that you don't know the cause of death?'

'No, sir,' answered Mr. Budd. 'I don't mean that at all. I know the cause of death all right — there's nothin' mysterious about that.'

'Then what do you mean, Superintendent?' The soft voice of Mahmoud Bey asked the question.

'I'll tell you what I mean, sir,' said Mr. Budd, and proceeded to do so.

They listened to what he had to say in amazement.

'But — but — ' protested Geoffrey Dinwater, when he had finished. 'It's not possible.'

The big man sighed wearily.

'We've all said that,' he murmured. 'And the answer is, it happened!'

'There are more things in Heaven and earth than the mind of man dreams of,' misquoted Mrs. Glibber suddenly and surprisingly.

'Meanin', ma'am,' said the superintendent, turning towards her, 'that Mr. Hayes was killed by somethin' supernatural?'

'There is no other explanation,' declared the woman with conviction.

'Nonsense, Annabel!' said her husband severely. 'To the scientific mind there is no such thing as the supernatural.'

54

She shot him an angry glance and shrugged her thin shoulders.

'Perhaps you can offer a better explanation,' she sneered — and there was a meaning in her voice that made the detective open his eyes sharply.

'Well,' remarked the stout man, 'I can't say I know enough about the supernatural to argue, ma'am. But a spook in a false beard doesn't sound convincin' to me.'

'The idea,' squeaked Glibber, 'is preposterous — completely preposterous!' He waved it out of existence with a gesture. 'There must be some practical explanation.'

'If you can think of one I'd very much like to hear it,' murmured Mr. Budd. 'In the meanwhile, I should like to ask one or two questions, if you don't mind.'

'What kind of questions?' murmured Mahmoud Bey softly.

'All sorts,' answered the stout superintendent. 'F'rinstance, did any of you hear anythin' unusual between half past twelve and one?'

'How could we?' snapped Mrs. Glibber. 'We were all in bed and asleep!'

'I wasn't asleep,' said Dinwater. 'The thunder woke me. But I heard nothing — nothing unusual.'

'Nor I,' said Washington Brown.

'And you, Miss Travers?' asked Mr. Budd, and the girl shook her head.

'Nor me,' put in Mahmoud Bey softly.

It was merely a routine question, and the big man had expected a negative result. If he himself and the watchful Leek had heard nothing, it was unlikely that any of these people would. He cleared his throat.

'Now, regardin' these Prophet letters,' he went on. 'Mr. Hayles took them more seriously than they seemed to warrant, and I am under the impression that he had a reason for that which he didn't disclose. Can anybody tell me what that reason was?'

There was a silence as he looked from one to the other, and then Washington Brown moved restlessly.

'Yes,' said Mr. Budd inquiringly, 'what is it?'

'I don't know whether I ought to tell you' — the secretary was hesitant — 'Mr.

Hayles expressly asked me not to mention it in case it should prejudice you. He had a strong suspicion who sent those letters.'

'Oh, he did, eh?' Mr. Budd was interested. 'And who did he think sent them?'

'A neighbour — a man who lives in Liddenhurst,' answered the secretary. 'He and Mr. Hayles have had several quarrels. He's a religious fanatic, and he thought that Mr. Hayles' profession was sacrilegious.'

'Do you mean the queer man?' broke in Inspector Hadlow.

Washington Brown nodded.

'Yes, that's the fellow.'

Mr. Budd turned quickly.

'Who is this queer man you're talkin' about?' he demanded.

'He's a peculiar chap,' said the divisional inspector. 'He lives in a cottage on the outskirts of the village. His name's Daniel Thane. But everybody calls him the 'Queer Man' in the district. He's a little bit touched, I think.'

'H'm!' commented the stout superintendent. 'And Mr. Hayles was under the impression that these anonymous letters came from him, eh?' He addressed the secretary, and Brown nodded. 'Why didn't he say so?' demanded Mr. Budd.

'Well, he wasn't sure,' replied Washington Brown. 'It was only because he'd had trouble with Thane before that he thought they might have come from him. But if his suspicions were wrong he didn't want to get the chap into trouble.'

'I've seen the man you're talking about,' put in Geoffrey Dinwater — 'tall, lean fellow. Goes about in sandals and a robe.'

'That's the man, sir,' said Inspector Hadlow. 'Eccentric, but I've always thought he was harmless.'

'Maybe he is,' remarked Mr. Budd. 'On the other hand maybe he isn't. Though I don't see how anyone, harmless or otherwise, got in and out of that room. Still, we ought to see him. How far away is this cottage?'

'About a couple of miles,' said Hadlow.

The superintendent looked at his watch.

'Gettin' on for three,' he murmured. 'I'd like to find out whether this feller's sleepin' or what he's doing.' He came to a sudden decision. 'We'll go along there. You can stay here, Leek. The rest of you can go back to your rooms. I'll see you in the mornin'. Nobody's to leave the house — understand that!'

He went out into the hall, followed by Hadlow, and beckoned to Murley, who was still lurking uneasily about.

'You can send the servants to bed,' he said. 'I haven't got time to see 'em now, and they'd better try and get some sleep.'

'Don't you think,' ventured Hadlow, 'we ought to leave seeing Thane until the morning?'

'No, I don't,' said Mr. Budd. 'I want to see him now. I want to know what he was doin' at the time Hayles was killed.'

He pulled open the massive front door and stared out into the rain-drenched night. The thunder was still muttering and rumbling, and the lightning played fitfully over the neglected grounds. With a resigned shrug of his shoulders the divisional inspector followed him to the waiting car and climbed up behind the wheel. Mr. Budd took his place beside him, and they drove off through the rain.

Except for the intermittent flashes of lightning the night was pitch-dark. There might be a full moon somewhere, but there was no sign of it, and the heavy thunderclouds shut out even the faint light that might have come from the stars.

The car hissed and splashed and bumped along the narrow road, the windscreen wiper working furiously, and the head-lights glittering on the downpour, so that the falling drops, as they came within their rays, looked like little globules of molten fire.

They sped through the sleeping village, ascended a steep hill, the wheels skidding and sliding, and came to a halt at the entrance to a footpath between a tangle of briars.

'We'll have to walk from here,' grunted the inspector. 'It's too narrow to take the car up.'

Mr. Budd got silently down and waited for Hadlow to join him. The inspector led the way along the narrow, winding track that passed through a dark coppice, and presently ended altogether in front of a tiny building, which was set in an oblong of garden. It was very small, and the big man drew in his breath quickly as he saw a glimmer of light shining dimly from behind a latticed window.

Hadlow led the way to a gate, opened it, and walked up a cinder path to the creeper-covered porch. A vivid flash of lightning illumined the scene, and Mr. Budd saw that the garden was full of old-world flowers that in daylight must have been a blaze of colour.

Hadlow reached the porch, and raising his fist, hammered on the door. There was a movement within, a shuffling step on bare boards became audible, and then the door was jerked open and the tall figure of a man, holding a lamp, peered out at them.

'Who comes at this hour?' said a deep voice. 'What do you want?'

'We'd like to have a word with you, Mr. Thane,' said Mr. Budd before Hadlow had time to reply. 'Mr. Reuben Hayles has been murdered!'

A pair of dark, hollow eyes turned on him.

'When did it happen?' asked a deep voice.

'Shortly before half-past one this morning,' answered the superintendent.

'Then the prophecy has been fulfilled,' said the strange man. 'Mohammed has struck down the desecrator of his grave! The vengeance of the prophet has fallen upon him!'

Never in his life before had the stout superintendent had such an extraordinary experience. There was something unreal, unnatural, about the whole situation. The thin, wild-looking figure of the man with the lamp, framed in the cottage doorway, the rumbling of the thunder, and the incessant flickering of the lightning, the monotonous hissing splash of the rain and the deep voice were like the component parts of some nightmare.

Hadlow must have felt something of the same sensation, for he seemed at a loss. It was Daniel Thane who broke the silence that followed on his last speech.

'Are you friends of Reuben Hayles?' he demanded, and Mr. Budd jerked himself out of the spell that had fallen over him.

'No,' he answered. 'We represent the police.'

'The police?' repeated the queer man, and there was no sign of apprehension either in his voice or face. 'Why, then, have you come to me?'

'Mr. Hayles,' said the fat detective, 'received several letters threatenin' him. From information received, we're under the impression that you wrote them.'

'Supposing that to be true, what then?' asked Daniel Thane.

'Then,' said Mr. Budd shortly, 'I should like an account of your movements between half-past twelve and half-past one this mornin'.'

'Are you labouring under the delusion,' said the queer man, 'that I am responsible for the death of this man, Hayles?'

'I don't know what I'm labourin' under,' said the stout superintendent irritably. 'But I want to know what you were doin', all the same.'

'I had no hand in Hayles' death,' said Daniel Thane, 'but I read it in the stars and in the music of the breeze. He died because he had violated the tomb of the prophet.'

'That may be,' said Mr. Budd. 'But

somebody killed him.'

'The hand of Mohammed killed him,' declared the queer man. 'It was written that Reuben Hayles should die, and he died.' He drew himself up, his gaunt figure in its curious monkish robe looking strangely dignified in the flickering light of the lamp. 'For the sake of knowledge, for the sake of worldly power and prestige, he violated sacred things. You tell me he is dead, and I am not surprised. Let others take heed and walk in the paths of righteousness and humility.'

'That doesn't answer my question,' said Mr. Budd stubbornly. 'I asked you what you were doin' between half-past twelve and half-past one!'

'I was out,' replied Daniel Thane. 'When the moon is at its full the spirits are abroad. The ancient goddess of Isis dances with Thor on such a night, and the souls of men can rise above the trivialities of mundane things and commune with the glories of nature.'

'Crazy as a coot!' murmured Mr. Budd below his breath, and looked a little helplessly at Hadlow.

He had dealt with all sorts of strange people during his long career, but Daniel Thane was completely outside his experience.

'During the time you were out did you go anywhere near the Manor House?' asked the divisional inspector, in an endeavour to answer the mute appeal in his confrére's eyes.

'Why should you question where I went?' demanded the queer man. 'Is not the country free to all who would enjoy its changing moods?'

'There's certain laws of property,' said the big man.

'I violate no laws!' retorted Daniel Thane. 'Neither the laws of man nor the laws of nature. But if you would speak further with me, come inside. My habitation is open to all men who are heavy laden.'

Mr. Budd was inclined to take this as a subtle reference to his stoutness, but he followed the other into the narrow passage, glad to get out of the rain, which was trickling coldly down his back.

The floor was bare of covering, but scrupulously clean, and the queer man led them into a room on the right. Here, also, was neither carpet nor linoleum, but the boards had been scrubbed to a whiteness that was dazzling. There was scarcely any furniture. A plain deal-topped table stood in the centre, and beside it a chair. Against one wall had been built a row of bookshelves, also of plain wood, containing several battered volumes. On another table near the window, rather to the big man's surprise, stood an ancient typewriter.

The sight of it set any doubts he might have had at rest. Old Reuben Hayles's suspicions had been correct. The letters that had so alarmed him had come from this strange individual who had set the lamp down on the centre table and was regarding them gravely.

'You are looking at my typewriter,' he said suddenly. 'A present from my niece, and an instrument that has been of inestimable value to me in my studies.'

'Very useful things,' said Mr. Budd. 'So you did write those letters to Mr. Hayles?'

'Why should I deny it?' answered Daniel Thane. 'I knew that death was

66

coming to him, and I warned him. I could do no more.'

'How did you know?' The superintendent adopted a conversational tone.

'It was revealed to me,' said the queer man. 'I was vouchsafed a vision.'

'But why did you send them anonymously?' inquired the fat detective. 'And post 'em in London?'

'Because I did not wish Hayles to know they emanated from me,' answered the other. 'Had he been aware of the source he would have ignored them. He was a self-willed, obstinate man.'

'You often go to London?' asked the superintendent.

'I go occasionally to visit my niece who works in a large store,' said Daniel Thane. 'I did not anticipate that my warnings would have any effect, but I hoped that they might prepare Reuben Hayles for the doom that was inevitable.'

Mr. Budd gently rubbed his chin. He was in something of a quandary. He lacked sufficient evidence to arrest this man for the crime, even had he believed him guilty, which he did not. To do so would necessitate endowing him with supernatural powers. But at least his visit had resulted in something. He had discovered the origin of the letters, and the discovery had satisfied him about one thing, and the new possibilities it gave rise to surprised and puzzled him. He wanted time to consider this extraordinary case from the fresh angle that his discovery had suggested.

In some respects it was alarming, and the problem how anyone got in or out of Reuben Hayles's bedroom was still unsolved. But it offered fresh material to work on.

There was nothing to be done with Daniel Thane at this stage of the inquiry, and they took their leave of that strange man. He accompanied them courteously to the door, and here Mr. Budd put his last question.

'Why did you sign those letters 'the Prophet'?' he asked casually.

The queer man surveyed him haughtily.

'Because,' he said gravely. 'I am a direct descendant of Mohammed!'

He watched them until they reached the gate, and then closed the door.

'Well, what do you make of that?' said Hadlow, as they set off to return to the car.

'The poor feller's barmy!' answered the big man briefly.

'I know that!' The divisional inspector was a little impatient. 'I mean do you think he's guilty of Hayles's murder?'

Mr. Budd shook his head.

'No, I don't think he's guilty,' he declared. 'He wrote those letters, and he certainly had a hand in the killing of Hayles, but I don't think he's guilty of murder.'

'You mean he's mad, and therefore not responsible for his actions?' said Hadlow. 'But still, I don't see — '

'That's true, but it isn't what I meant,' answered Mr. Budd cryptically.

And all the way back to the Manor House the divisional inspector tried to discover some sense out of this contradictory assertion, without success. If ever Hadlow had been relieved to have a murder investigation taken out of his hands, it was now.

6

Find the Motive

The storm ended with the coming of daylight, and dawn brought a clear sky and the prospect of a fine day. The police photographers arrived just after it was light, and for some little while there was the popping of magnesium flares in the death-room, and the acrid odour of burnt powder.

When they had gone the body of the archaeologist was removed to a waiting ambulance and taken to the mortuary to await the inquest. Divisional Inspector Hadlow went back to the station to make his report, and Mr. Budd, accompanied by the melancholy and yawning Leek, went out into the sunshine for a tour of inspection.

He satisfied himself that the oak tree grew too far away from the house for anyone, however active, to have used it as a means of reaching the study window. Neither was there any means by which the wall could have been scaled. There was no ivy here, and nothing that offered a hand or foothold.

'I keep tellin' yer,' protested Leek wearily, as he watched his superior conduct this examination, 'that nobody could 'ave come this way! I was within a few yards of the place the 'ole time, and I'd 'ave 'eard 'em!'

'You may have been in a trance!' grunted Mr. Budd.

'You've never found me neglectin' me duty!' said Leek indignantly. 'I was as alert last night as I am at midday!'

'Then I should think a regiment of soldiers could have come by you and you wouldn't 'ave noticed 'em!' retorted Mr. Budd unkindly.

The long-suffering sergeant sighed.

'You will 'ave your little joke,' he said aggrievedly. 'But seriously, I tell yer, no one could 'ave come this way without me seein' 'em.'

The big man was prepared to believe it. He went in from his fruitless search and interviewed the servants, but he learned nothing. The rest of the household were not up, and after an early breakfast he settled himself in the drawing room to consider the position.

He felt certain that so far as the anonymous letters were concerned, they could be eliminated. They had, in his opinion, nothing to do with the death of old Reuben Hayles beyond suggesting it to the murderer. That was the new angle that had occurred to him during his interview with the queer man. Daniel Thane had sent those letters purely as the outcome of a delusion, and the person who had killed the archaeologist had seized upon them as a screen behind which he or she could carry out their crime. At least, that was the theory that Mr. Budd was working on.

Daniel Thane might be crazy, but he was not a killer. The big man could not imagine him killing anyone, much less could he imagine him wandering about in a false beard. That, he felt, was the crux of the whole business.

He had examined the beard carefully,

and discovered that it was not even made of real hair. It was a very bad beard; the kind of trumpery thing that one uses at Christmas. It would have been obviously false if anyone had worn it. And yet the murderer had worn it, and the old man had, apparently, torn it off just before he died. There was no other way to account for its being found in his hand.

Discarding the letters as having any bearing on the archaeologist's death brought up a fresh question. What was the motive? Originally it seemed that he had been hailed by some crazy fanatic because he had violated the tomb of Mohammed. But according to Mr. Budd's new theory this didn't still hold good. Therefore, he had been killed for some other reason. What was it? If he could discover the motive, then the identity of the murderer shouldn't be difficult, and that brought him once more to the principal problem. How had the crime been carried out?

It was useless finding the murderer until he could explain that. The killer could afford to snap his fingers. 'You say,'

Mr. Budd could hear him remarking triumphantly, 'that I killed Hayles. Prove it! Show how it was possible, in the circumstances, for anybody to have killed him!'

And that was his strong suit. Until that could be answered satisfactorily he was safe — safe even though everyone in the world knew him to be guilty.

The big man threw away the butt of the cigar he had been smoking and lighted another. What had promised to be a very boring business had turned out to be remarkably interesting. Someone had taken advantage of the threatening letters for their own purpose; had even made a profitable use of the presence of Mr. Budd himself. Behind the murder of the old man was a cunning brain, and the stout superintendent, the more he thought of it, the more uneasy he became. The pattern was not yet complete. At the back of his mind he had an unpleasant feeling that there was more to come — that this killing of the archaeologist was only an item in the scheme, which had been hatched by the unknown.

However, his visit to Daniel Thane had

led to something. He was no longer hampered by those anonymous letters. He might have wasted a lot of time on them. Now he was free to devote his inquiries elsewhere.

Just before lunch Reuben Hayles's solicitor arrived. He was a jovial, red-faced man, not in the least like the usual conception of a lawyer. The stout man learned that Washington Brown had telephoned for him.

'This is a dreadful thing — a terrible thing!' he said, when Mr. Budd had a private interview with him. 'Have you any idea who could have been responsible for the poor old fellow's death?'

The big man shook his head.

'Not at the moment, but I'm rather glad you're here, though, because you may be able to help me.'

Mr. Kinman looked at him in mild surprise.

'In what way?' be demanded.

'Well, I'm anxious,' explained Mr. Budd, 'to discover a motive, and the most likely motive is money. Was Mr. Hayles a rich man?'

'It depends,' said the cautious lawyer, 'what you consider a rich man. Reuben Hayles was very well off. Everything considered, I suppose he was worth about two hundred thousand pounds.'

Mr. Budd whistled softly.

'I'd call that almost a millionaire,' he murmured. 'Who gets all this money, sir?'

The solicitor smiled and shook his head.

'I'm afraid that's not going to help you,' he said. 'Everything goes to his niece, Miss Travers, and I don't think you could suspect her.'

Mr. Budd scratched his chin.

'No, I don't think I can, sir,' he admitted. 'Not because she's a girl and pretty, but because this crime was carried out by somebody more powerful. I doubt if she'd have the strength to administer a blow like what killed Mr. Hayles. So she gets all the money does she?'

'Yes. I have the will with me,' replied Mr. Kinman.

'And did she know she was goin' to get it?' asked the fat detective.

The lawyer shook his head.

'No. She had no idea!' he declared. 'The only people who knew were myself, Mr. Hayles and the secretary, Brown.'

'H'm!' said the big man disappointedly. 'Well I don't think that's goin' to help me a lot. Had Mr. Hayles any enemies?'

'Every man has enemies,' retorted the solicitor sententiously. 'But I know of no one who hated Hayles so much that they would wish to kill him.'

And on this unsatisfactory note the interview ended.

The big man had to admit that he was completely at sea. With the exception of the beard he had no clue at all to the identity of the killer. Neither could he find a motive, which might have given him a pointer.

What was the reason behind the old man's death? He had exhausted money, and vengeance seemed unlikely. What remained? Jealousy?

He rambled about the neglected grounds after lunch smoking cigar after cigar, irritable and depressed, and he was coming despondently back to the house with the intention of going to his room for a short rest, when he saw Murley looking anxiously about. The butler caught sight of him at the same moment, and came quickly towards him.

'I've been trying to find you, sir,' he said, and his face was drawn and worried. 'I've found something important.'

'What is it?' asked Mr. Budd hopefully.

'If you'll come with me I'll show you, sir,' said the big-nosed man, and led the way into the house.

He ascended the staircase, passed along the corridor in which Mr. Budd, on the previous night, had kept his vigil, and paused outside a door at the far end.

'This is Miss Travers' room,' he whispered. 'She's downstairs in the drawing room at the moment. Come in.' He turned the handle softly, entered, and waited for the stout Superintendent to join him. 'This is what I wanted to show you, sir,' he said in the same low tone.

Going over to a wardrobe he opened it, pulled aside some dresses that were hanging neatly on hangers, and pointed. Mr. Budd stooped and peered in the direction of his finger. On the bottom shelf of the wardrobe were a number of shoes, but it was not these that caught his eye and riveted his attention. It was a square, iron weight that bore on the side a large 3, followed by the letters lbs.

A three-pound weight that was covered with blood!

7

Suspects Narrowed Down

Mr. Budd stared at the sinister object for a second or two without speaking, then he looked at Murley.

'How did you come to find this?' he asked.

The butler passed the tip of his tongue over his dry lips.

'The cook missed it, sir,' he said. 'It's usually kept in the kitchen. We use it as a doorstop. The door between the kitchen and the scullery is badly hung, and unless you have something to prevent it, it swings to of its own accord. Very inconvenient it is when you're busy and in a hurry. We looked for it, but we couldn't find it anywhere, although it had been there yesterday. It was Milly, the housemaid, who discovered it here. Miss Travers had spilt some grease on a pair of white shoes, and she gave them to Milly to try to get it off. When she came to put them back she saw this and noticed the blood. She was scared and frightened, and told me. I made sure she hadn't been imagining things, and came to find you, sir.'

'Did she touch it?' asked Mr. Budd sharply.

The butler shook his head.

'I asked her that,' he said, 'thinking of fingerprints.' He smiled faintly. 'I read a lot of detective stories in my spare time,' he explained. 'Never imagined that I'd have a crime on my own doorstep, so to speak.'

'H'm!' grunted Mr. Budd. 'You haven't mentioned it to anybody else?'

'No, sir. Only the servants know, of course.'

'Well, go down and tell 'em to say nothing,' said the big man sharply.

'You don't think — ' The butler hesitated. 'You don't think Miss Travers could have — '

'I don't think anythin'!' broke in Mr. Budd untruthfully, for he was thinking lots of things and very rapidly. 'Go and do as I tell you.'

Murley departed rather reluctantly, and when he had gone the stout superintendent gingerly lifted the weight out of the wardrobe by the crossbar at the top. There was a magazine on the table by the bed, and this he brought over, placed it on the top of a dressing table by the window, and stood the weight on it.

There was no doubt that this was the weapon that had struck that terrible blow which had killed old Reuben Hayles. The blood had dried, and in it were several grey hairs. And it had been found in Kathleen Travers's wardrobe.

He frowned at it, rubbing his massive chin. The girl had had the motive, but it was impossible to imagine that she could have had strength enough to wield such a heavy thing. Impossible to imagine it even if she could explain how she had done it.

His mind went back to the previous night. He remembered her passing him in the passage and going into her room. She had not come out again. How, if she was guilty, had she succeeded in committing the murder?

Back once more, he thought grimly, at

the old problem. How? How? How?

Was it possible there did exist some means of communication between this and Hayles's bedroom? Some other entrance than the door and the window?

Mechanically he shook his head. It was impossible! If there had been anything of the sort the careful inspection that they had made would have revealed it. No, if Kathleen Travers was responsible for the death of her uncle she had planned the crime with superhuman ingenuity, planned it so well that it was impossible to conjecture how she had done it.

He tore the middle out of the magazine and carefully wrapped the weight in it. The girl would have to explain how that incriminating object had got where it had been found.

He came out of the room softly, closed the door, and walked rapidly along the corridor. On the landing he met Geoffrey Dinwater coming up the stairs.

'Hello!' said that vacuous young man. 'How are things going? Have you discovered anything?'

'Well, we're followin' up a line of

inquiry,' said Mr. Budd evasively. 'But we've got nothin' definite yet.'

'How did you get on with old Thane?' asked Dinwater.

'He's a queer fellow,' replied the big man. 'But I don't think there's any harm in him.'

'He's queer enough,' remarked the other. 'Got religious mania, or something. He came here once, and there was a devil of a row. Tried to show uncle the error of his ways. Said that all this opening of graves was sacrilegious, and that vengeance would certainly overtake him if he continued.'

'He talked like that when I saw him,' said Mr. Budd. 'But he's loony! I'd like a word with you, Mr. Dinwater, in private.'

The young man raised his eyebrows.

'Come up to my room,' he said. 'I was just going to do a little work.'

Mr. Budd followed him up to the second landing and into a room at the beginning of the corridor, similar to the one below. It was an extremely untidy appartment, but more comfortably furnished than the other bedroom. An easy chair was drawn up near the grate, and a large table littered with books and papers stood in the window.

'I'm rather keen on mathematics,' said Dinwater, waving his hand towards the table.

'And on detective fiction, apparently, sir,' remarked Mr. Budd, eyeing a book-case that was stuffed with a number of crime novels.

Dinwater smiled.

'That's my relaxation,' he said. 'You've got to have something after a course of higher mathematics. What did you want to see me about?'

'I take it,' said Mr. Budd slowly, 'that you live here permanently?'

The other nodded.

'Yes, that's right,' he said. 'Both Kathleen and I. Our mothers were Uncle Reuben's sisters. They're both dead now. The old man was very decent, he sort of adopted us.'

'I see,' murmured Mr. Budd. 'And you were always on friendly terms with him?'

Dinwater eyed him keenly.

'Look here,' he said, 'what's the idea

behind these questions?'

'Nothing, sir,' said Mr. Budd sooth-ingly. 'Just that I want to acquire all the information I can.'

'Well, yes,' said the other. 'Uncle was a little eccentric, but we got on with him fairly well. He was away a lot, of course.'

'There was no trouble at all?' persisted the stout man.

'Why? Why do you ask that?' asked Dinwater sharply. 'Has somebody been talking? There was nothing in that. I dare say uncle would have come round in time.'

Mr. Budd had no idea to what he referred, but he thought it best not to appear ignorant.

'You think he would?' he said doubt-fully.

'Of course he would. He had nothing against the man. It was only that I think he was under the impression Kathleen was too young to consider marriage.'

The fat detective felt a sudden quickening of his pulses. Here was something! But it had to be handled carefully or Dinwater as a source of information would dry up.

'Well, maybe he was right,' he said.

'I don't know,' replied Dinwater frowning. 'She's of age, and surely entitled to choose her own husband.'

'It depends upon the choice,' said Mr. Budd.

The other nodded.

'I believe you're right,' he said. 'I think that had a lot to do with the trouble. Uncle was queer and old-fashioned in many ways. He thought Tinsdale wasn't — well, rich enough!'

Now, who's this feller Tinsdale? thought Mr. Budd.

'A doctor, especially a newcomer, hasn't got much chance of a practice in Liddenhurst,' went on Dinwater. 'Although I think Arthur Tinsdale's a clever fellow, and will make his way in the world. Who told you about the quarrel?'

'I heard of it,' said the big man evasively.

'That old cat, Annabel, I'll bet!' grunted Geoffrey Dinwater. 'The scandal-mongering old busybody! She made it worse by butting in and siding with uncle.

That's really what got Kathleen all worked up.' He lit a cigarette and flung the match into the grate. 'You can take it from me,' he said, 'that that's got nothing to do with uncle's death. Kathleen's got a temper, but she doesn't mean half she says. You'll find this fellow Daniel Thane at the bottom of the whole business.'

'Well, I shall be very glad to find someone at the bottom of the business,' remarked Mr. Budd wearily. 'At the present moment I don't see any bottom to it at all.'

'No, it's a pretty ticklish problem,' said Dinwater. 'I've puzzled over it a lot. The difficulty is, of course, how the murderer escaped.'

'And how he got in,' supplemented the fat man. 'Yes that's the difficulty, Mr. Dinwater. Maybe you can work it out mathematically?'

The other looked at him seriously.

'Maybe I can,' he said.

'Well, if you do, you might let me know,' said Mr. Budd, and took his departure.

He had learned something fresh and

something important. There had been a quarrel between Kathleen Travers and her uncle over a doctor, Tinsdale, who, apparently, had a practice in Liddenhurst. Old Reuben Hayles had obviously objected to the marriage of these two. And Tinsdale was penniless.

Here was a further motive for the girl to wish her uncle out of the way. With Hayles dead she became the possessor of a large fortune, and the freedom to marry the man she wanted to. It was a strong motive, and coupled with that blood-stained weight, Milly, the maid, had discovered at the bottom of her wardrobe, was sufficient, in any ordinary circumstances, to warrant an arrest. But, and here Mr. Budd swore softly below his breath, but — how had she managed to do the impossible? And why had that false beard been found in the dead man's hand?

It was incredible to suppose that the girl had worn a beard, not only incredible but ludicrous. The big man had a strong sense of humour, and in his mind's eye he could visualise Kathleen Travers with that atrociously obvious false beard. It was ridiculous!

All the same, she had the motive, and the weapon had been found in her room. A thought struck him. Was it possible that this Doctor Tinsdale was guilty?

Had he been the wearer of the beard? Were he and the girl in it together?

This was probable. It was more than probable, if — and again the big man swore gently to himself — if it could be found how he had managed to do the impossible.

8

Mr. Budd Works it Out

The divisional inspector called after tea to inform Mr. Budd that the inquest had been fixed for the Tuesday morning, and to the astonished Hadlow the big man related the further discoveries he had made.

'It looks pretty serious for the girl,' commented the inspector when he had finished. 'I know this man Tinsdale. Quite a respectable, hard-working young fellow. When he's got any work to do,' he added. 'He bought old Withers's practice when he died. But I should think he was pretty nearly at the end of his tether. Most of the patients in the neighbourhood had only kept on with Withers out of sentimental reasons, and they were only too anxious of the excuse to go over to Johns. This place isn't really big enough for two doctors, and Johns gets all the plums. I happen to know that Tinsdale owes money right and left. There's certainly motive enough there, considering the money the girl'll come into now Hayles is dead.'

'There's motive enough,' said Mr. Budd irritably. 'It isn't that that's worrying me, Hadlow. It's the method.'

The inspector nodded.

'Yes, that's the stumbling block, sir,' he agreed. 'I've thought and thought until my head aches, but I can't see any explanation.'

'That's where our hands are tied,' muttered Mr. Budd. 'We can't do anythin', Hadlow. We can't arrest anybody until we can explain how they could have killed the old man. There must be somethin' we've overlooked.'

'I suppose' — the divisional inspector was a little diffident — 'I suppose your sergeant didn't fall asleep, or anything?'

'No. I can vouch for him,' said the stout superintendent — an assertion that would have gratified Sergeant Leek immensely had he been there to hear. 'If he says nobody came by the window, nobody did!

Apart from which, I must have been in the room three seconds after the blow was struck. And the first thing I did was to go to the window. I should have seen anybody!'

Hadlow shrugged his shoulders.

'Well, there it is,' he said dubiously. 'Somebody killed the old man, and they killed him with that weight. I suppose Dr. Scavage's suggestion isn't feasible at all?'

'You mean that it was flung through the window?' said Mr. Budd, and shook his head. 'How far d'you think you could throw a three-pound weight, Hadlow? And how are you goin' to get it back again after you've thrown it?'

'It might have had a string attached to it, or something like that?' suggested the inspector, but again Mr. Budd shook his head. 'You try pullin' a three-pound weight out of an open window by a piece of string,' he said. 'It would have fallen on the floor, and you've got to pull it up over the sill. It couldn't be done.'

'Well, it's the only thing I can think of,' sighed Hadlow, 'unless' — he smiled a little wanly — 'that woman downstairs

— Mrs. Glibber — was right, and it's something more than the mind of man dreams of.'

'Bosh!' said the man crossly. 'Don't you go gettin' all spiritualistic and psychic. There's a natural explanation, same as there is to anythin', if we can only find it.'

'If we can only find it!' echoed Hadlow dubiously.

Mr. Budd rose to his feet with an unaccustomed access of energy, and his fist came down heavily on the table.

'We've got to find it, and we're goin' to find it!' he declared. 'There's nothin' that happens that isn't possible of an explanation, and this has happened. We've got a dead man in the mortuary to prove it! And we've got a blood-stained piece of iron.'

'And we've got a false beard,' murmured the divisional inspector.

'And we've got a false beard!' agreed Mr. Budd. 'And all we've got to do is to connect 'em up, You've got a man watchin' Thane?'

Hadlow nodded.

'Well, you'd better put another on to

watch Tinsdale, and a third to keep an eye on this house and see that nobody tries to do a bunk,' said Mr. Budd rapidly. 'I don't know anythin' definite yet, but I'm not takin' any chances. Maybe we're all wrong. Maybe that feller Thane is at the bottom of the business. Maybe his disembodied spirit came in through the window, bashed old Hayles on the head, and slipped out through the keyhole! Maybe he employed Isis or Thor, or some of his queer friends, and got a spook to pop that weight into Kathleen Travers' wardrobe. Maybe — ' He stopped suddenly. 'Maybe!' he ended in a peculiar voice.

'What have you thought of?' asked Hadlow.

The interview was taking place in the big main bedroom, and he stared thoughtfully at the foot of the bed.

'I don't know,' he said slowly, and his energy slid from him like a cloak, leaving him sleepy and lethargic. 'I dunno. I've got somethin' poppin' in my head.'

He became so absent and distrait from that moment that the divisional inspector curtailed his visit.

'I shall be at the station if you want me,' he said, as Mr. Budd accompanied him down the stairs.

'Maybe I will want you later,' murmured the stout man thoughtfully. 'If I can find the 'how', I shall certainly want you.'

'The how and the why,' said Hadlow; but the big man shook his head.

'I think I've found the why,' he remarked. 'Both the why and the who. Yes, I think I have. It's the how that's beating me. But maybe I'll find that, too.'

They had reached the deserted hall, and Hadlow glanced at the big grand-father clock that was solemnly ticking.

'Good lord, I'd no idea it was so late!' he declared. 'I've got an appointment at seven, and it's nearly half-past six now. What's the matter?'

For Mr. Budd was staring at the clock as though he'd seen a ghost.

'Eh?' The stout man turned. 'Eh? What did you say?'

'What were you staring at?' demanded the divisional inspector. 'Did you see something?'

'Yes, I saw somethin',' agreed Mr. Budd, and there was a queer, excited note in his voice. 'I saw somethin'. I think it's likely you'll be gettin' that telephone call, after all.'

*　*　*

Sergeant Leek, having been left to his own devices, elected to go for a walk. It was warm and pleasant, and the country surrounding the Manor House was worth exploring. He strolled along leafy lanes and broad highways, through woods and across commons, a lean, melancholy figure in his rather shabby suit of blue serge.

In his own fashion he enjoyed himself, although no one seeing him would have imagined so for an instant. He had rather the appearance of having just left the funeral of some near and beloved relation. His long face wore an expression of settled melancholy, and his sad eyes surveyed the beauties around him without apparent enthusiasm.

He found a little teashop on the outskirts of Liddenhurst, and came back in the calm of the evening while the church bells were ringing, fervently hoping that Mr. Budd had not been requiring him. But when he reached the Manor House there was no sign of the big man. He was not in his bedroom, and he was not in the grounds. He appeared to have disappeared.

Dinner was over, for which the sergeant was thankful. These meals in which you all sat round the table and stared at one another, embarrassed him. He liked eating alone and in comfort. He had brought in a packet of sandwiches, and, going to his room, he munched them comfortably.

It was funny where the 'sooper' had got to. Perhaps he'd gone down to the inn after beer. The sergeant strongly disapproved of alcoholic drink.

He finished his frugal meal, and picked up an old magazine, which he found in the room. He was still reading when at half-past nine the door opened and Mr. Budd came in.

'Where have you been to?' he demanded. 'I've been lookin' for you everywhere.'

'I didn't think you'd want me, so I went for a walk,' answered Leek. 'Was it anythin' important?'

'Oh, no!' said Mr. Budd sarcastically. 'Just an inquiry into this murder.'

'Well, I'd been 'angin' about all day,' said the sergeant, 'and nobody seemed to want me. Why didn't you say there might be somethin' doin'?'

'I was afraid it might interfere with your evenin's enjoyment,' said the stout superintendent. 'I want you to find all the people stayin' in this house, with the exception of the servants, round 'em up in the drawin' room, and keep 'em there until I tell 'em they can go.'

'What's up?' demanded Leek curiously.

'The balloon will be pretty soon!' said Mr. Budd complacently. 'Now, get along downstairs and do as I tell you.'

*   *   *

The divisional inspector was on the point of going home when the telephone call, that Mr. Budd had suggested might possibly occur, came through.

'I've got it all worked out,' said the slow, sleepy voice. 'If you'll come along up to the Manor House I think I can show you how the impossible can be made possible.'

'D'you mean you've discovered the how?' said Hadlow excitedly.

'I think I have,' answered Mr. Budd. 'Come along up.'

The inspector was interested and lost no time. The call had come through at a quarter past ten, and at half-past he was talking to Mr. Budd in the latter's room.

'It's very simple,' said the stout superintendent. 'It was the clock that gave me the idea.'

'The clock?' repeated Hadlow. 'How in the world could that tell you? I don't see how a clock can explain a person making himself invisible.'

'No, I don't suppose you do,' said the superintendent. 'As a matter of fact, it doesn't. The person didn't make himself invisible.'

'Then what did he do?' said the exasperated Hadlow. 'If he wasn't invisible somebody would have seen him.'

'Anybody could have seen him,' said Mr. Budd, a slight twinkle in his sleepy eyes.

'But nobody did see him,' protested the baffled inspector. 'You didn't see him and Sergeant Leek didn't see him.'

'We didn't see him,' explained the superintendent, 'because we didn't look in the right place. If we'd looked in the right place we should have seen him all right. He didn't do anythin' supernatural. But he did do something that was remarkably clever.'

Hadlow's patience was exhausted.

'Well, tell me,' he said. 'How did he get in and out of that room without being seen?'

'He didn't!' said the fat detective, with irritating calmness. 'He didn't get in and out of that room without bein' seen for the very simple reason that he was never there!'

9

The How and the Why

The divisional inspector stared at the complacent Mr. Budd in stupefied bewilderment.

'But if he wasn't there,' he protested, when he could find his voice, 'how did he kill Hayles?'

'There you are, that's the clever part of it,' said the stout man. 'He not only killed Hayles, but he left his beard behind.'

Hadlow made a gesture of despair.

'I give it up,' he said.

'Well, I'll give you a practical demonstration,' said Mr. Budd. 'Come along to the study.'

He took the inspector downstairs, turned into the corridor, and taking a key from his pocket unlocked the door of the room in which old Reuben Hayles had met his death. He reached for the switch.

'Now,' he said, as the light came on,

'take a look round. The place is exactly as it was last night.'

Hadlow looked round keenly and discovered that the stout superintendent's words were true. With the exception of that sprawling figure on the rug, the room was exactly the same. Even the window had been opened. He went over to it, and looked out. In contrast to the previous night the sky was clear and the moon was just rising, a round yellow ball low on the horizon, rather like a gigantic Chinese lantern.

'Well,' he said, 'what next?' as Mr. Budd stood silently by and watched him.

'Next,' said the fat detective, 'I'm goin' to ask you to sit down on the edge of the bed there, and whatever happens you're not to move. Now listen very seriously to this, Hadlow. Whatever happens, don't move! If you do, you may get hurt.'

'All right,' promised the inspector. 'I won't move. What are you going to do?' he asked in surprise, as his companion went ponderously to the door.

'I'm goin' to leave you for a minute or two,' said Mr. Budd, 'and by the time I come back you'll know just how Reuben Hayles died.'

He disappeared, shutting the door behind him, and the bewildered Hadlow was left alone. He took his seat gingerly on the edge of the bed and stared about him, wondering what was going to happen next. There was something queerly uncomfortable about sitting in that lighted room in which a man had come by his death, waiting.

There was scarcely a sound in the house. The screech of an owl from outside came faintly to his ears, but nothing more. Dead silence!

He looked at the oblong patch that marked the window and instinctively he felt that the phenomenon he was about to witness would come from there. And presently it did. Swiftly and without warning.

He heard the faintest rustle, and then a black object came hurtling through the open window — a silent, rushing missile.

With an exclamation, Hadlow half started to his feet, and then there was nothing. The window was blank once more.

The inspector's pent-up breath left his lips in a harsh sigh. He had seen, and yet he still didn't understand. The thing had come and gone with lightning speed. He was itching to go to that open window and look out, but he remembered Mr. Budd's words and remained where he was, stifling his curiosity and trying to curb his impatience.

A footstep sounded in the corridor, the handle turned softly, and the big man came into the room.

'Well,' he said, 'did you see it?'

'I saw it,' said Hadlow. 'What was it?'

'Three pounds of hard iron,' answered Mr. Budd grimly. 'The thing that struck Reuben Hayles and crushed the front of his skull like an eggshell.'

'But what happened to it?' demanded Hadlow. 'I still don't understand.'

'Well, now come with me, and I'll show you the neatest murder machine that was ever conceived by the brain of man.'

'Where are we going?' muttered the inspector.

'Upstairs again,' said the stout superintendent,

Hadlow thought they were going back to his room, but he quickly discovered that this was not their destination. Mr. Budd paused before he reached it, opened a door on the right, and signed to his companion to enter. The inspector did so.

'Whose room is this?' he demanded.

'The room of the man who killed Hayles,' said Mr. Budd, 'It's immediately over his bedroom, as I expect you've guessed. Now look here.'

He went over to the open window, and Hadlow saw, resting on the floor, the iron weight attached to a thin, strong wire.

'See that hook?' said Mr. Budd, pointing to a hook that had been screwed into the top of the window frame. 'I put that there. He'd taken away the one he'd used last night, but the hole was there.'

Still Hadlow didn't quite understand, although a glimmer was seeping into his brain.

'Don't you see?' said Mr. Budd. 'Look at the oak tree.'

'What's the oak tree got to do with it?' demanded the inspector,

'He fastened the weight to the end of the wire,' explained the big man carefully, 'and measured the wire so that when the other end was attached to this hook the weight hung down so that it was exactly level with the head of a man of the height of Reuben Hayles standing in the window below. And then he took a piece of twine, fastened that, too, to the weight, passed it over that branch of the oak tree, and brought the end of the twine back to the window of his room. Then he pulled the whole thing up out of sight among the leaves. Got me?'

Hadlow nodded.

'All he had to do,' went on Mr. Budd, 'was to wait until the victim was standin' in the window below and cut the twine. The weight came rushin' down with almost the force of a bullet on the end of its wire, swung in through the open window, and hit Reuben Hayles a smashin' blow on the forehead. The force of the blow sent him staggering backwards, and he collapsed in the middle of the room. The weight, of course, immediately swung out again, and the man waitin' above pulled it quickly up. There was nothin' to be seen. Nothin' but a dead man in the room below, and no means to show how he'd been killed.'

'Good lord! What a diabolical arrangement!' breathed Hadlow, and Mr. Budd nodded.

'Yes, it was diabolical and clever,' he said.

'But,' the inspector frowned, 'how did he insure that Hayles would go to the window? He might not have gone near it, or the window might have been closed.'

'He knew the window wouldn't be closed,' said Mr. Budd. 'I've been talkin' to Murley, and I understand that it was Mr. Hayles' habit to leave that window open day and night in all weathers. How he arranged for certain that Hayles would go to the window, is, I think, one of the cleverest touches of all. You remember the beard?'

Hadlow, who in the excitement had forgotten, stared.

'The beard?' repeated Mr. Budd. 'The false beard. He hung it on the end of a thread and dropped it down so that it would swing in the open window. Naturally, when Hayles came into the room and put on the light, and saw such an extraordinary thing danglin', he went over to examine it. He had it in his hand when the weight was released, and that's why it was there when we found him.'

'But why a beard?' said Hadlow.

'Why not?' retorted Mr. Budd. 'I think he had at the back of his mind an idea that he would clutch the beard and have it in his hand when he was found. It 'ud help to create the illusion which he wanted — that someone had actually been in the room and struck the blow.'

'But when was all this arranged?' said the inspector. 'It must have been prepared beforehand. He must have needed a ladder to get up the oak tree.'

'Oh, yes!' said Mr. Budd. 'It was all prepared beforehand. It was all waitin' there right through Saturday. But the wire and the thread were so fine that you couldn't see them unless you were lookin' for 'em. And who would expect to look for such a thing?'

'And who — who occupies this room?'

He looked round.

'The feller we're goin' down now to arrest,' said Mr. Budd. 'The fellow who planned not only one murder, but two. There was another one in his mind, but it wasn't goin' to look like murder. It was goin' to look like justice. The man who tried to frame Kathleen Travers by puttin' that weight in her wardrobe — Mr. Geoffrey Dinwater!'

* * *

Mr. Budd sat in the Assistant-Commissioner's office on the Monday afternoon and listened with gratification to the words of praise which Colonel Blair had offered in connection with his efforts at Liddenhurst.

'The astounding thing to me,' said the grey-haired, dapper man, 'is that you cleared the whole thing up in such a short time. Excellent work, Superintendent — excellent!'

The big man's heavy face flushed faintly.

'I thought at one time I was goin' to fall down on it,' he said. 'And I believe I would have done if it hadn't been for the clock.'

'The clock?' said the puzzled Assistant-Commissioner, who had heard nothing about a clock.

'There was a grandfather clock in the hall,' explained Mr. Budd. 'One of those big things with weights and a pendulum. I'd just found that three-pound weight, and was puzzlin' over the mystery of that room, when I saw the pendulum, and it gave me the idea.'

'Dinwater, of course, was after the money,' said Colonel Blair.

'Oh, yes!' answered the superintendent. 'The money was at the back of it. When he confessed, after we'd cornered him and shown him exactly how he'd done the trick, he admitted that he'd got into a hell of a mess with moneylenders, and worse things, and didn't know which way to turn. Then his uncle showed him one of them stupid letters from Thane, and he began to wonder if he couldn't use it as a cloak for his own ends.'

'But the whole object was to implicate the girl,' said the colonel.

'The object was general mystification and a good alibi for himself,' corrected Mr. Budd. 'The girl could be attended to after. With her out of the way he became next of kin, and naturally the money would have gone to him.'

'But I don't see,' protested the Assistant-Commissioner, frowning, 'how be was going to get the girl out of the way. Until you discovered how the trick was worked, you couldn't have arrested her, and once you'd discovered that, it was obvious who'd done the murder.'

'I don't think,' said the big man slowly, and his face was grave, 'that he was altogether relyin' on our arrestin' her. I've got an idea from somethin' he said that Kathleen Travers would have committed suicide, or so it would have appeared. And everybody would have thought she'd done it because she was guilty.'

'Good heavens!' Colonel Blair stared. 'You mean that Dinwater would have — '

'I think he would,' broke in the superintendent, nodding. 'He was a nasty piece of work — a very nasty piece of work! But he was clever — I will say that.

It was one of the neatest ideas I've ever come across.'

His fingers went mechanically to his waistcoat pocket, and he produced a cigar before he remembered where he was. Rather embarrassed, he was putting it back when the Assistant-Commissioner stopped him.

'Smoke if you want to,' he said generously, and with a sigh of content Mr. Budd stuck the cigar between his lips and felt in his pocket for his matches.

THE VANISHING MEN

1

The Man Who Vanished

Mr. Budd climbed ponderously out of the train at Marley Halt and looked sleepily about him. The little station was primitive — a strip of wooden platform; a microscopic shelter — and set in the middle of open country. Meadows and ploughed fields, interspersed with great patches of woodland, stretched away in all directions as far as the eye could see.

Sergeant Leek, his long, melancholy face wearing its habitual expression of abysmal gloom, joined his superior on the platform, and the train moved on.

'I s'pose this is the right place,' grunted Mr. Budd. 'Can't see any sign of a village, can you?'

The lean sergeant shook his narrow head.

'Maybe it's somewhere over there among them trees,' he said, pointing vaguely.

'Maybe it is,' growled Mr. Budd, 'an' maybe it's in another direction altogether. Or p'r'aps it's vanished, too! Let's see if we can find somebody who knows.'

He moved off slowly towards the small shelter into which he had seen the aged porter, who had signalled the train on, disappear.

'Oughtn't someone to 'ave met us?' said Leek, as they walked along the platform.

'They ought, but they haven't,' replied Mr. Budd, transferring his shabby suitcase from one podgy hand to the other. 'There's Methuselah. He'll tell us how to get to Shepton Magna.'

He called to the elderly porter who was just entering the tiny booking office. The old man turned and surveyed him with rheumy eyes.

'Can you tell me the way to Shepton Magna?' asked Mr. Budd; and the ancient porter stared at him vacantly.

'Eh?' he wheezed.

'Which is the way to the village?' said the stout superintendent.

'Wot do 'ee say?' The porter shuffled

closer and put a gnarled hand up to his ear.

'Deaf as a post!' snarled Mr. Budd disgustedly. 'He would be!'

He bellowed his question again in a stentorian voice that must have been audible a mile away. The porter's wrinkled face assumed an injured expression.

'There's no call for to shout,' he said indignantly. 'I ain't deaf — only a little 'ard of 'earing! You wants to get to the village?'

Mr. Budd loudly signified that he did.

'Well, yer goes out o' the station and yer turns to the left,' said the old man. 'Yer keeps along the road till yer comes ter Boyle's Farm. Then yer bears to the right by the pond an' keeps on up the 'ill, an' then yer takes the third on the left till yer sees the crossroads. There's a signpost there, and yer can't go wrong.'

Mr. Budd groaned.

'How far is it?' he demanded.

'Eh?'

'I said how far is it?' roared the superintendent.

119

'Well, as the crow flies, a matter of two mile,' replied the porter.

'I'm not a crow!' snarled the big man. 'By road, I mean.'

'Nigh on four mile,' said the porter with great satisfaction. 'Yus, close on four mile it must be.'

Mr. Budd looked at the dejected Leek.

'Four miles!' he grunted. 'Round by the pond, round by the farm, up the hill — Good Lord! We shall be dead before we get there!'

'I used to do a lot o' walkin' in me youth,' remarked Leek reminiscently, and was withered with a glance.

'And look what it's done for you!' snapped Mr. Budd. 'Isn't there a bus, or somethin'?' He turned again to the porter.

It took some time for the question to penetrate to the old man's brain, but when it did he shook his head triumphantly.

'No, there ain't nuthin' of the sort!' he declared. 'I allus uses me bicycle.'

'Fat lot o' good that is to us!' growled the big man. 'Four miles! Why can't they build the infernal station nearer, instead of sticking it down in the middle of nowhere? Oh, well, I s'pose we'd better get started — '

He stopped as the sound of a car reached his ears, ambled ponderously out of the shelter, and peered down the steep slope to the road. A rather dirty and dilapidated-looking Ford had come to a halt at the foot of the incline, and a red-faced man with the appearance of a farmer was getting out.

'Hi!' called Mr. Budd. 'Are you going to Shepton Magna?'

'Is that Sup'ntendent Budd, of Scotland Yard?' inquired the red-faced man; and when the stout superintendent grunted an affirmative: 'I'm Inspector Mumble, of the Norwich Constabulary. Afraid I'm a bit late, but I 'ad a bit o' trouble with the car and — '

'Better late than never!' said Mr. Budd hastily. 'I'm very glad to see you. I don't think I've ever been so glad to see anybody before.'

Inspector Mumble looked rather astonished at the warmth of his greeting.

'If you'll come and get in the car, sir,'

he said, with a gratified grin, 'we'll get along. I've booked rooms for you and your sergeant at the Shepton Arms, an' the chief constable 'ull be waitin' to see you.'

'Come on, Leek.' Mr. Budd lumbered heavily down the slope and threw his suitcase into the car, squeezing his ample form in beside it. When the lean sergeant had taken his place Inspector Mumble started the engine with some difficulty and they drove off, followed until they were out of sight, by the curious eyes of the grizzled old porter.

Shepton Magna proved to be a small, old-world village with quaint little shops lining its cobbled High Street, and a scattered collection of labourers' cottages grouped about its oblong green.

There was an ancient church surrounded by a churchyard and flanked by a red-roofed, ivy-covered vicarage. The place had escaped the march of progress and remained very much the same as it had been in those dark ages when many of its inhabitants had been burned at the stake for practising witchcraft.

The Shepton Arms was a low, rambling building of yellow-white stone, with leaded windows and a tiled roof, facing the green, and as Inspector Mumble brought the decrepit Ford to a noisy stop in front of the entrance a man, who had been standing in the narrow doorway, came forward to meet them.

'Superintendent Budd? I'm Colonel Wrayford.' He introduced himself pleasantly. 'Come along inside. I've ordered some food for you. And I expect you can do with it after your journey. Eh?'

Mr. Budd was grateful. He could do with it. They had left London very early that morning, and the journey had been both long and tiring.

The table had been laid in the bar-parlour, a low-ceilinged room full of old-fashioned furniture, and nothing was said about the business that had brought them to Shepton Magna until after they had eaten and drunk the excellent food and beer which the Shepton Arms had supplied. And then the grey-haired chief constable took a long pull at his tankard and set it down.

'This is a very queer business, Superintendent — a very queer business indeed,' he began.

'I gathered it was something out of the ordinary, sir,' replied Mr. Budd, applying a match to the end of one of his black cigars. 'But, of course, I know very few of the details. I understand four people in the district have disappeared under mysterious circumstances?'

Colonel Wrayford nodded.

'Under very mysterious circumstances,' he said, with emphasis. 'Inspector Mumble has all the details. I think it would be best if he were to give you a summary of what has happened, and then we can hear your views and exchange ideas.'

Mr. Budd agreed, and the red-faced inspector produced a large notebook, and cleared his throat.

'The first of these 'ere disappearances took place eight weeks ago,' he began, his eyes on his notes.

'Thomas Hardiman, a farm-labourer, living in a small cottage just outside the village, came 'ome from his work as usual at six o'clock on the evening of the tenth of March. 'E had a wash an' 'is tea, and at a few minutes before 'alf-past seven started out to walk down 'ere for a drink, an' a game o' darts. He's never been seen since!'

Inspector Mumble paused and looked across at his London colleague, but Mr. Budd had apparently gone to sleep.

'On the eighteenth o' March, which was a Sunday,' he continued, in a slightly louder tone, 'Dr. Hickthorne, up on the Green, was called out at twelve o'clook at night to visit a woman at one of the cottages at the other end of the High Street wot was expecting a baby. 'E arrived there at 'alf-past twelve, and left just before two, during which time the child was born. But 'e never reached 'is 'ome, an' from that day to this nobody ain't set eyes on 'im. On the twenty-seventh of March,' went on the inspector, 'Mr. Alec Kilfoyle, Sir David Kilfoyle's son, what lives in Shepton Manor, back o' the church, drove down before dinner to collect a parcel from the station at Marley Halt. He didn't come back to dinner, an' 'e didn't come back at all. His car was found up by Boyle's Farm, with one of the back tyres flat, an' the parcel what 'e'd been to fetch on the seat; but there wasn't no sign of Mr. Kilfoyle, an' there ain't been no sign of him since.'

Again Inspector Mumble sought for some trace of interest on the part of Mr. Budd; but that mountainous man was slumped back in his chair motionless, and, seemingly, unconscious. The inspector looked at the chief constable, from him to the lugubrious Leek, and continued:

'The last of these disappearances took place on the second of April. George Pilcher, a lad of eighteen, employed at the vicarage, went over on 'is evening off to visit 'is young lady, who's in service at Fenbridge, the next village to this 'un. He left 'er to walk back at ten o'clock, and that's the last that's ever bin seen of 'im.'

'Interestin' and peculiar,' murmured Mr. Budd, partly opening his eyes. 'Was there any connection between these people?'

'Well, they knew each other by sight, and possibly to speak to,' answered the chief constable; 'but that's all. There was nothing between them that would explain them vanishing like this.'

'Very queer,' said the big man, stifling a yawn — 'very queer indeed! And you've discovered nothing?'

'Nothing at all,' replied the colonel, shaking his head. 'Mumble has done his best, but nothing's come to light. These people have just vanished without rhyme or reason, as far as I can see. It was because we were up against a blank wall that I decided to call in the help of Scotland Yard. Something had to be done.'

'What has been done?' asked Mr. Budd.

'A description of the missing men has been circulated,' replied Mumble, 'and every railway station within a 'undred mile 'as been visited, and inquiries made. We've searched the country, and dragged all the ponds an' suchlike, but we 'aven't found a single thing. It almost makes yer think there's somethin' in what people is sayin'.'

He uttered the last sentence slowly, and a little hesitantly.

127

'Nonsense! Nonsense!' snapped the chief constable testily. 'That's ridiculous — absurd!'

'What are people sayin'?' inquired Mr. Budd lazily.

'Well,' Colonel Wrayford frowned, 'this place is very old, you know, and the inhabitants are steeped in superstition. In the old days the district used to be a hotbed of magic and witchcraft. Even now — well, I understand that quite a number still believe in such things. There's a rumour about that these disappearances mark a revival of Black Magic. It's a lot of nonsense, of course.'

'The first thing we've got to decide, as far as I can see,' said Mr. Budd, making no comment about the local rumour, 'is whether anything's happened to these four people at all.'

'I don't understand you.' The chief constable looked puzzled. 'They've vanished, and — '

'Yes, sir, I know,' broke in the stout man. 'But have they vanished of their own accord, or is somebody responsible for 'em vanishin'?'

'Why should they have vanished of their own accord?' demanded the colonel. 'I don't think we need take that possibility into consideration.'

'I think we ought to take everythin' into consideration,' said Mr. Budd stubbornly. 'It's not impossible that these four men have disappeared for reasons of their own. They may have known each other more intimately than anyone knew. P'r'aps they was mixed up in some business together, or somethin' like that. I'm not sayin' they was, but, seein' that we don't know anythin', we've got to consider everythin'!'

'I see your point,' said the chief constable. 'But I think it's very unlikely that these men had anything in common. What do you say, Mumble?'

'I agree with you, sir,' said the inspector. 'I can't see anything that 'ud be likely to link four such different fellers together.'

'Well, somethin' has linked 'em,' said Mr. Budd, 'or they wouldn't have vanished like they have. I s'pose there's nothin' known against 'em? They weren't in any sort of trouble or difficulties?'

The inspector shook his head.

'We 'aven't found nothin' of the kind,' he answered. 'Hardiman an' Pilcher was straight, 'ard-workin', honest chaps and — '

He broke off as there came a tap on the door, and a flushed, excited face was thrust into the room.

''Scuse me,' said a voice hoarsely; 'but I knew you was 'ere, sir, and — '

'Come in, Selter!' interrupted Mumble. 'What is it?'

The door was pushed open, and Mr. Budd saw that the face belonged to an excited and breathless policeman.

'There's a body bin found — in the pond by Boyle's Farm,' said the police-man. 'Some kids saw it, an' — '

'A body!' snapped the chief constable. 'Whose body?'

'One of these fellers we've bin lookin' for, sir,' said the agitated policeman, drawing a deep breath. 'Tom Hardiman.'

2

Three More to Die?

There was a little group of curious sightseers collected round the pond near Boyle's Farm when Mr. Budd, Leek, the chief constable, and Inspector Mumble reached it, and they scattered to make way for the newcomers. A constable, a confrére of Selter's, was standing stolidly beside a sodden, shapeless bundle that lay on the grass edging to the pool of weed-covered, brackish water. He saluted stiffly when they came up to him. The inspector began to question him in a low voice, and Mr. Budd peered down at the body. It was not a very pleasant sight. From its appearance the stout man concluded that it must have been in the water for a considerable time. The face was puffed and bloated, and the clothing covered with slimy mud and weeds.

'Horrible, isn't it?' muttered Colonel

Wayford at his elbow.

'It's not very pretty, sir,' admitted Mr. Budd. 'I s'pose there's no doubt that it is this feller Hardiman?'

'Why — what makes you ask that?' said the chief constable quickly.

'Well, it seems to me,' answered Mr. Budd sleepily, 'that it 'ud be difficult to say who it is in the condition it's in.'

Colonel Wrayford scratched his long chin doubtfully.

'I don't know — Selter seemed sure,' he said. 'I never met the man, so I can't say. Mumble knew him, and, of course, his wife will be able to confirm his identity.'

'It's Hardiman right enough, sir.' The inspector had joined them in time to hear sufficient to guess what they were talking about. 'Those are the clothes he was wearing when he disappeared, though he's in a pretty bad state, isn't he?'

'Dreadful!' said Wrayford. 'It's rather strange, don't you think, that, since he must have been in the water so long, he wasn't found before?'

'I was thinkin' that,' said Mr. Budd,

slowly. 'And this pond was dragged, too, wasn't it?'

'Yes,' answered Inspector Mumble. 'But not since three weeks ago.'

'Exactly,' murmured the big man, 'and this poor feller disappeared on the tenth of March. That's eight weeks ago. Where was he between then and the time he was put in the pond?'

'I see what you mean.' The inspector's sandy eyebrows drew together. 'Yes, it's queer!'

'He must have been somewhere durin' those five weeks,' continued Mr. Budd. 'Where the others went.'

The chief constable made a distasteful grimace.

'The whole thing's horrible!' he said. 'There's something — beastly about it! Why did these men disappear? Where did they go? Why was Hardiman killed? There's no motive. It's sheer lunacy!'

'It's always been my experience, sir,' said Mr. Budd soothingly, 'that lunacy very seldom proves to be at the bottom of this sort of thing. There's always a motive somewhere. It's our job to find out.

This'll be the doctor, I s'pose?'

A small car, driven furiously, came to a stop with a squeaking of brakes, and a middle-aged man with a nose like the beak of a parrot got out and hurried towards them.

'I'm Dr. Kyle,' he announced curtly, his small, narrow eyes darting swiftly from one to the other. 'You telephoned — '

'That's right, sir,' said the inspector. 'I telephoned.'

He explained the situation briefly, and the doctor listened, pursing his thin lips. 'H'm, found in the pond, was he?' he muttered. 'I wonder if the others will be found now, in similar circumstances? It's a most extraordinary business. I knew Hickthorne, of course, quite well. He came over several times to Fenbridge in consultation. H'm, well, I suppose I'd better have a look at this fellow. Can't do much, you know. There'll have to be a post-mortem, naturally.'

Still keeping up a running commentary under his breath he knelt beside the body and made his examination.

'H'm, been in the water some time

— there's a wound here on the head — pretty severe one — probably fractured the skull — h'm — h'm — been dead well over three weeks, I should say — impossible to say what caused death — might have been drowning — we shall see when we look at the lungs — h'm, well, that's all I can do at present.' He came to his feet and faced them.

'You can move him now,' he said. 'Have you sent for an ambulance?'

Inspector Mumble nodded.

'Selter is bringing it up,' he replied. 'How much over three weeks would you say this feller had been dead, doctor?'

'Difficult to tell,' said the doctor, shaking his head. 'The body's in an advanced state of putrefaction. I'll be able to answer that question after I've made a post-mortem.'

'Could he have been dead as long as eight weeks?' inquired Mr. Budd gently. The doctor swung round and stared at him for a moment before he replied.

'I should doubt it,' he said after a little consideration. 'No, I should say not more than five weeks at the outside.'

'Thank you,' murmured the big man. He rubbed his massive chin thoughtfully, went over to the body, and stooping, began cautiously to search the pockets. It was a difficult and a not very enviable task, for the clothing was sodden and muddy. He found nothing at all. All the pockets were empty, and he was straightening up, breathing heavily from his exertion, when a small coupé drove up and stopped.

A man's head peered curiously out of the side window and then the door was opened and the owner of the head got down on to the roadway. Mr. Budd eyed him sleepily as he approached, and saw a man of medium height with a slightly florid complexion and a neat, carefully trimmed moustache that lay along his upper lip like a smear of black paint.

'What's the trouble here?' he inquired in a high-pitched voice, as he came up to them.

'Just found Tom Hardiman's body in the pond, sir,' answered Inspector Mumble respectfully, and Mr. Budd concluded from his tone that the newcomer must be someone of importance.

'Tom Hardiman, eh?' The florid-faced man peered shortsightedly at the shapeless bundle on the ground. 'Is he dead?'

'Yes, sir, I'm afraid he is,' said Mumble.

'And you found him in the pond — how did he get in the pond?' asked the other quickly.

'That's what we want to know, sir,' replied the inspector.

'It's a funny business,' grunted the newcomer. 'When was it he disappeared? Eight weeks ago, wasn't it? Has he been in the pond all that time?'

'No, he has not,' said Mr. Budd. 'He certainly has not!'

The stranger gave him a quick, searching glance, and Inspector Mumble appeared to think that an introduction was advisable.

'This gentleman is Mr. Osborne, who owns Boyle's Farm,' he said. 'Sup'n'tendent Budd 'as come from Lun'un to 'elp over these disappearances.'

'I hope you'll be successful, Superintendent,' said Mr. Osborne. 'What do you think of our mystery? Extraordinary business, isn't it?'

'I'm ready to agree with you, sir,' said the big man. 'An' this doesn't make it any the less extraordinary. I'm wonderin' whether the others 'ull turn up in the same kind o' way?'

'Do you think that's likely?' said the chief constable, who had been speaking to the doctor and rejoined the group in time to hear Mr. Budd's remark.

'I don't see why not,' said the stout superintendent slowly. 'Four people have vanished in similar circumstances, and one comes back dead. It seems very likely to me that the other three'll do the same.'

'But what motive could anyone have for spiriting away four such totally different people and then killing 'em?' demanded Mr. Osborne.

'That's what we've got to find out, sir,' answered Mr. Budd. 'Yes, that's it — in a nutshell — the motive. Once we've got that, we'll have the person who's at the bottom of this.' He pursed his thick lips and nodded sleepily.

'If there is a motive,' muttered Colonel Wrayford dubiously.

'There's a motive for everythin',' said

Mr. Budd tritely. 'People don't just vanish into thin air an' turn up again in ponds without a reason. That's not sense!'

'It's not sense, anyway,' remarked Mr. Osbome. 'It's just sheer, crazy lunacy!'

At that moment Selter appeared with the ambulance, and under the curious eyes of the whispering sightseers the unpleasant remains of poor Tom Hardiman were carried to the primitive conveyance and wheeled away.

Mr. Budd yawned.

'Well, I don't see that there's much more to be done here,' he remarked. 'You'll be draggin' the pond, of course, Inspector?!

Mumble, who had not had any intention of doing anything of the kind, stared at him for a moment blankly and then nodded.

'Of course,' he agreed.

'You might find somethin', you never can tell,' went on the stout man. 'The body must 'ave been weighted with somethin', otherwise it 'ud come up before. Maybe those weights 'ud be interestin'.' He turned to the chief constable. 'I'd like a word with the relatives of these people who've vanished, sir,' he said, 'an' I'd like to start with Sir David Kilfoyle.'

'We'll go straight up to the manor from here,' said Colonel Wrayford. 'Sir David will, I know, be very glad to see you. He is, naturally, extremely upset and worried over the disappearance of his son, and it was at his urgent entreaty that I agreed to call in the assistance of Scotland Yard.'

He had a hurried word with Inspector Mumble and carried Mr. Budd off to the waiting car.

'Who's that feller Osborne?' asked the big man as they started back towards the village.

'He's a writer,' answered the chief constable. 'I understand that he's writing a history of the county, and Shepton Magna in particular.'

'Bin here long?' murmured Mr. Budd inquisitively.

'No, about three years, I think,' said the colonel. 'That's considered nothing in these parts, you know. Most of the people here have lived here for the whole of their lives, and their parents before them. I don't know a great deal about Osborne — why?'

'I'm naturally of a curious disposition,' said Mr. Budd evasively, and closing his eyes did not open them again until the car stopped in front of the imposing entrance to a large mansion which the chief constable, rather unnecessarily, informed him was Shepton Manor.

In answer to their ring the massive oaken door was opened by a black-clad servant who bowed as he rocognised Colonel Wrayford.

'Will you come in, sir,' he said, ushering them into the big hall. 'Sir David is in the library. I will tell him you are here.'

He closed the door and went away. Mr. Budd occupied the ensuing interval by taking sleepy stock of his surroundings.

There was money here. Its evidence was visible on every hand. The rugs, the pictures, the furniture, were all expensive, but there was no blatancy. It was all old, good stuff; as old as the house itself. A movement on the big staircase attracted his attention and he saw that a woman was slowly descending. As she came into the light he saw, also, that she was young and very pretty. She gave them a quick, curious glance as she crossed the hall to a door on the left, and disappeared into the room beyond. Mr. Budd eyed the closed door thoughtfully. His deceptively sleepy gaze had seen something else mingled with that look of curiosity. A faint apprehension, or perhaps — fear.

'Who was that?' He murmured the question softly to the man at his side.

'Miss Linley,' replied the colonel. 'She's engaged to Arthur Glenton, Sir David's nephew.'

The soft-footed butler reappeared at that moment to inform them that Sir David Kilfoyle would see them. They were conducted to a long, low-ceilinged room lined with bookcases and occupied by two men, the elder of whom was standing with his back to the great carved fireplace.

He was a thick-set, stockily built man, with an almost completely bald head and rather prominent blue eyes. The other man, who was lounging in a deep armchair, was thin and dark and much younger.

'Come in, Wrayford — come in!' grunted the stocky man. 'Well, have you any news?'

'So far as your son is concerned, I'm afraid not,' said the chief constable. 'This is Superintendent Budd, of Scotland Yard, Sir David, and — '

'How d'you do? Very glad to see you here.' Sir David Kilfoyle interrupted the chief constable's introduction, and turned to Mr. Budd. 'Now, perhaps, we shall get to the bottom of this dreadful business — eh?'

'I hope so, sir,' said Mr. Budd, thinking that this was not a very tactful way of putting it, considering the chief constable's presence. 'I hope so. I shall do my best.'

'The whole thing is inexplicable!' declared Sir David, and his round face puckered into a worried frown. 'Nobody could have had any reason for harming my son.'

'Or any of these other people, apparently,' said Wrayford; 'and yet somebody has harmed poor Hardiman. His body was found a short while ago in the pond at Boyle's Farm.'

Sir David Kilfoyle went suddenly white.

'Good lor'! How dreadful!' he whispered huskily. 'I thought that all the ponds and ditches in the neighbourhood had been searched?'

'So they had, sir,' said Mr. Budd, 'but he wasn't there then.'

'If he wasn't in the pond then, where was he?' The dark man spoke for the first time.

'That's what I'd very much like to know, sir,' said Mr. Budd. 'That's a very pertinent question. Yes, sir — where was he? He disappeared eight weeks ago, and his body was found today. The doctor says he couldn't have been dead more'n five weeks. What happened to him durin' the other three weeks?'

'And what has happened to the other two and my son?' muttered Sir David, passing a shaking hand over his bald head. 'Where are they?'

The stout superintendent guessed the

fear that lay behind the question and tried to offer consolation.

'Maybe they're where Hardiman was before he was put in the pond,' he said. 'Maybe nothing's happened to 'em.'

He had very little hope that what he said was right, and apparently Sir David thought the same, for he shook his head.

'I'd like to believe that,' he answered. 'I want to believe it, but I can't! I believe they are dead, too.'

He spoke calmly, but it was only by a great effort.

'Don't look on the black side, Uncle David,' said the younger man. 'Perhaps the superintendent's right.'

'What is your idea about this devilish business?' asked Sir David, turning swiftly towards Mr. Budd. 'What do you think can be at the bottom of it?'

The big man shook his head.

'At present I haven't an idea, sir,' he replied candidly. 'I haven't even started thinkin' yet. Before I begin to get ideas I want to know a lot more than I do now.'

'You know as much as we do,' grunted the chief constable.

'That's where you're wrong, sir, if you'll pardon me saying so,' said Mr. Budd. 'I don't know as much as you do. F'rinstance, I never knew any of the people concerned, or their friends an' relations, or anythin' about 'em. Until I've got into the skin of 'em, so to speak, if you understand what I mean, I wouldn't start formin' theories.'

'And how long do you suppose it will be before you do start?' demanded Sir David Kilfoyle in a tone that suggested he was not very impressed by this bovine, sleepy-eyed man before him.

'Quicker than what you'd think, sir,' said Mr. Budd. 'I'm very — what's the word? — sensitive, that's it — I'm very sensitive to atmosphere.' He stifled a yawn, and then went on: 'Now there's one or two questions I'd like to ask you, sir, if you don't mind.'

'Ask anything you like,' said Sir David promptly. 'I'll give you all the help I can — which, I'm afraid, is not much. My only anxiety is to discover what has happened to my son.'

Mr. Budd's 'one or two questions' was

an elastic term, for he subjected Sir David to a close examination concerning his son that lasted altogether nearly an hour and a half.

'I think that's all, sir,' he said, with a weary sigh, when he had exhausted his subject. 'I'm sorry to have bin so long,'

'Time doesn't matter,' declared Sir David impatiently, 'so long as some result is achieved.'

'I suppose it has occurred to you,' said his nephew, getting up and lighting a cigarette, 'that these disappearances may be the work of a lunatic?'

'Yes,' answered Colonel Wrayford, 'we've considered that possibility.'

'It seems to me the only plausible explanation,' continued Arthur Grenton. 'Don't you agree, Superintendent?'

Mr. Budd rubbed his chin and screwed up his thick lips into a pouting circle of doubt.

'I'd rather not express an opinion at the moment, sir,' he murmured, 'but maybe you're right.'

'What do you want to do now?' asked the chief constable, when they had taken their leave and rejoined the waiting car.

'Well, sir,' said Mr. Budd thoughtfully, 'I'd rather like to go back to that pub. The beer was very good — some of the best I've ever tasted — an' I think an evening spent in the bar 'ud be both pleasant and instructive.'

Colonel Wrayford said nothing, but he wondered, if these were the usual methods adopted by Scotland Yard, how any results were ever achieved at all!

3

The Barn

Mr. Budd found Sergeant Leek, a miserable and unhappy man, waiting for him when he reached the Shepton Arms.

'Where did you get to?' asked the sergeant, a little resentfully. 'I never saw the goin' of you. One minute you was there, and the next you wasn't.'

'I've been gettin' acquainted with the people in this business,' said his superior, 'or, at any rate, some of 'em.'

'You might 'ave taken me with you,' said Leek, in an injured tone. 'I looked a proper fool in front of that inspector feller.'

'Well, I couldn't help that,' retorted Mr. Budd. 'That's Nature's fault, not mine. To be perfectly candid, I forgot all about you!' He dipped a fat finger and thumb into his waistcoat pocket, and produced a cigar. 'This is one of the queerest jobs we've ever bin on — from what I can see of it,' he continued ruminatively, carefully removing the band. 'One of the queerest, an' one of the most difficult.'

'Why, what 'ave you found out?' asked the sergeant.

'That's just it; I haven't found out anythin',' said Mr. Budd, frowning. 'It struck me that this Alec Kilfoyle, bein' the only rich feller of the four, might somehow supply the reason for this epidemic of vanishin'; but now I've heard all about him, I don't see how he can. He seems to 'ave been a very ordinary chap. No trouble over money, or women, or anythin'. And he certainly hadn't got anythin' to do with Hardiman or Pilcher, though 'e did know Dr. Hickthorne. No, it's a complete puzzle, an' I don't quite know how to begin on it.'

This was such an amazing admission for Mr. Budd to make, that it rendered Leek completely speechless. He tried desperately to think of a brilliant suggestion, and the effort contorted his lean face into such an anguished expression that his superior looked at him in alarm.

'What's the matter?' he asked. 'Aren't you feelin' well?'

'I was just trying to think — ' began the sergeant.

'Don't you go takin' risks like that,' advised Mr. Budd. 'Remember there ain't no doctor nearer than that feller Kyle, at Fenbridge, an' by the time he got here it might be too late. Come into the bar an' have a lime-juice. P'raps it'll put you right.'

He led the way, and Leek followed in silence, knowing from experience that it was useless to utter any protest when it pleased his superior to wax facetious.

When Mr. Budd had informed the chief constable that he proposed to spend the evening in the bar of the Shepton Arms, he had been quite serious. There was, as he very well knew, no better place for picking up local gossip than the bar of a village pub. Tongues become loosened, and it is possible to learn more about the lives of the inhabitants, their reaction to one another, and the general opinion concerning local events in a couple of hours than in a week of questions.

151

The Shepton Arms was no exception to the rule. The bar was full and buzzing with talk when they entered, for the news of the finding of Tom Hardiman's body had spread rapidly. Ignoring the whispering and the curious glances that were directed towards him, Mr. Budd went to the bar and ordered a tankard of beer for himself, and a lime-juice and soda for Leek, who never drank anything stronger. He carried these to a secluded corner, and settled down to listen.

For a little while the talk was subdued owing to their presence, but after a bit they were forgotten, and it became more natural. It was apparent that Tom Hardiman had been well liked. Several of his friends seemed to be present, and there was much gloomy shaking of heads over his death. The subject of the disappearances was freely discussed, and it gradually became evident to the listening Mr. Budd that, whereas Hardiman, young George Pilcher, and Alec Kilfoyle had been popular, Dr. Hickthome had not. There was nothing apparently definitely against him; he had been clever at his job, and always ready to turn out at any hour of the day or night to attend a case of sickness, no matter who it was. But his manner had been brusque and offhand, and he had failed to endear himself to the villagers.

There was no doubt at all that the disappearances had given rise to great uneasiness throughout the village — an uneasiness that had been enhanced by the discovery of Hardiman's body. There was, too, an undercurrent of fear that was in a large measure due to superstition.

One man — he was the local sweep — went so far as to declare openly that someone had put a spell on the neighbourhood.

'And,' he added, staring darkly into his tankard, 'it wouldn't be difficult to put a name to 'em neither.'

'Meanin' Osborne, o' Boyle's Farm, I s'pose,' said a small, scraggy-necked man.

'No names, no pack-drill,' put in a stout man, in a greasy cap, with a warning glance in the direction of Mr. Budd and the sergeant, but the sweep took no notice.

'Ay, that's the feller!' he said, nodding.

'Things ain't never bin the same since 'e come. 'Member wot 'appened the week arter 'e bought the farm?'

There was a general murmur and nodding of heads.

'All them cows bein' took sick an' dyin' wasn't nat'ral — I don't care wot no one says,' went on the sweep, frowning. 'And again there was them crops o' Fenlocks. Turned black, they did — 'member?'

'Ay; and that was followed by the death o' old Belton — found dead in 'is own turnip field!' said the scraggy-necked man. 'It's true enough, Jim. There 'as bin a rare lot 'o trouble in these 'ere parts since that feller bought the farm.'

Mr. Budd listened with interest. He was learning more by just sitting still and listening than he would have done by a week's questioning. Obviously these people did not like the owner of Boyle Farm. Certain things had happened since he had arrived in the district, for which they blamed him. It was, of course, ridiculous to suppose that he had had anything to do with the deaths of three cows and the rest, but there must be some reason why these villagers had settled on him as the cause. That was the interesting part. He took a sip from his tankard, and continued to listen to the conversation going on around him.

'There's queer things goes on at the farm, you mark my words,' said the sweep darkly. 'Why's that there big barn all lit up at night? Can any of yer tell me that?'

Nobody apparently could, since they made no attempt to answer him.

'Blazin' from dark till dawn,' continued the sweep. 'An' why? That's wot I'd like ter know. Why?'

'P'r'aps that's where 'e does 'is writin',' suggested the man in the greasy cap.

'Why should 'e do it in the barn?' demanded Jim. ''E's got the 'ouse there to do it in, ain't 'e? An' why only now an' again? It ain't lit up every night. Only once a month. An' d'yer know when that is?' He paused and lowered his voice. 'On the night when the moon's full.'

Mr. Budd felt a sudden creepy little chill in the region of his spine. He knew the significance attaching to that last remark, and, in spite of the cosy surroundings of the Shepton Arms, a momentary superstitious fear took possession of him.

London, with its lights and its noise, seemed at that moment very far away. He was back in the dark ages, when anything was possible. It was only for an instant that he experienced this queer sensation, and then he was once more his old phlegmatic, practical self.

There was a silence after the sweep's remark, broken at last by the scraggy-necked man.

'There's a full moon tonight,' he said meaningfully.

'An' that there barn 'ull be lit up till the risin' o' the sun,' declared the sweep. He swallowed the remainder of his beer and banged the empty tankard on the counter as a signal for it to be replenished.

'What do yer say ter us goin' along, then, an' findin' out what 'e's doin'?' said the man in the greasy cap, looking from one to the other.

'Not me!' retorted the sweep, shaking his head. 'There's some things wot is best left alone, Charley — an' that's one of 'em.'

'Four people 'ave vanished already, mate,' said the man with the scraggy neck soberly. 'Best not go interferin' with things wot is agin Nature. I ain't never bin near Boyle's Farm arter dark, an' I wouldn't — no, not fer all the money in the world!'

There was a chorus of agreement.

'Well, what d'yer say to a game o' darts?' said the man called Charley. 'I'll take Bill, an' play you an' George for a pint.'

'That's on!' agreed the sweep with alacrity. 'An' yer may as well get yer money ready, Charley. It's a walkover.'

It was; and they played another game, which Jim and his partner also won. By this time it was getting on for ten, and the landlord was preparing to shut for the night.

'Well,' murmured Leek, draining his glass of lime-juice. 'I s'pose we may as well pop off ter bed — an' I can't say I shall be sorry. Travellin' always makes me tired.'

'Everythin' makes you tired,' said Mr. Budd, 'so there's no need to blame the

157

railway. But you ain't poppin' off to bed just yet.'

The sergeant's face lengthened.

'Why not?' he asked. 'There ain't anythin' more we can do ternight.'

'There's a lot *I* can do tonight,' interrupted his superior. 'An' you're goin' to help me. I'm rather anxious to see this village by moonlight.'

'What for — ' began Leek.

'Because I'm naturally romantic,' said Mr. Budd, 'An' there's nothin' like a moon — an' particularly a full moon — to give me ideas. Not the sort of ideas it gives some people,' he added. 'An', anyway, I couldn't get sentimental with you.'

Leek sighed. He had been rather looking forward to his bed.

'It seems a silly idea to me,' he remarked dolefully.

'Then it's very probably a good one,' grunted the stout superintendent, 'because you nearly always get everything upside down. Come on we'll go before they shut the place.'

He rose to his feet and strolled over to the bar.

'I'm just goin' to have a little walk before turnin' in,' he said to the landlord.

'Then you'd better take the key of the side door, sir,' was the reply. 'It's never bolted, only locked. Will you be wantin' anything when you come in?'

'No, thank you,' said Mr. Budd, and when the key had been found and given to him, left the bar, followed by the unhappy sergeant.

'Which way are we goin'?' asked Leek, as they paused outside the inn.

'I should have thought that even you would have had sense enough to know that,' said Mr, Budd soothingly. 'We're going up to Boyle's Farm to see if this barn is lit up tonight.'

'Surely you wasn't takin' no notice of what those fellers was sayin'?' protested the surprised sergeant. 'An ignorant lot of yokels — '

'Yokels they may be; ignorant they certainly are not,' retorted the big man. 'They've got some sense — an' that's where they differ from you. Anyway, we're going to Boyle's Farm.'

The sergeant relapsed into silence and

trudged along beside his fat companion with weary resignation.

There may have been a full moon somewhere, but it was not visible. The sky was a mass of cloud that made the night dark and chilly. It was only possible to see a few yards ahead, and they had to go warily, for they were not familiar with the way.

It seemed to Leek that they had been walking for miles before they came in sight of the pond from which the dead body of Hardiman had been taken, and Mr. Budd stopped to take his bearings.

'The place should be over there,' he muttered, pointing.

'I can't see anything,' answered Leek, straining his eyes into the darkness.

'Did you expect it to be outlined in electric light like a picture house?' grunted Mr. Budd. 'Of course you can't see anything. I can't see anything myself, but I know it's somewhere there.'

He began to walk in the direction he had indicated, and presently the building loomed into view — a blot of deeper darkness against the darkness of the sky.

It was a low-roofed, rambling place set about with trees, and flanked by straggling outbuildings.

The big barn mentioned by the sweep was about fifty yards from the house itself, a bulky structure, with a pointed roof, and it was in complete darkness.

'There you are!' said Leek mournfully. 'Didn't I tell you?'

'You didn't tell me anything worth hearing,' said the big man. 'You never have. It's early yet. Maybe they haven't started their tricks.'

He stood in the narrow roadway, and looked about him. The entrance to Boyle's Farm was set between high, unkempt hedges — a heavy gate in which he was just able to make out a small wicket. Going over, he tested this gently. It was locked. Coming back he rejoined the lugubrious sergeant.

'How long do you intend stopping here?' said Leek, thinking of his cosy bed at the Shepton Arms.

'I don't know,' grunted Mr. Budd. 'Maybe we'll stop here a long time, maybe we won't. It just depends.'

The sergeant devoutly hoped that whatever it depended on wouldn't happen.

There was a chill wind, and it was unpleasant standing in the gloomy little lane, staring at a dark mass that showed no sign of life at all. His own opinion was that they were just wasting their time; but he kept this to himself, since long experience had taught him that it was quite useless to argue with the big superintendent when once he had got an idea firmly fixed in his mind.

A clock, somewhere in the village, chimed eleven, and almost coincident with the last note a sound came to their ears from behind the locked gate of the farm. It was very faint, and scarcely audible, but in the silence unmistakable — the opening and closing of a door.

Mr. Budd held his breath and strained his ears, but there was no other sound. Then, quite suddenly, a light sprang out of the darkness. It came from a square window, set high in the black bulk of the barn — a powerful light that shone steadily. The big man eyed it speculatively. So the gossip of the villagers had not been entirely without truth.

Mr. Osborne, or somebody, had left the farm, and gone into the barn. The stout man rubbed his chin thoughtfully. It would be interesting to know what was going on inside that lighted building. He began to seek a means of satisfying his curiosity. With a whispered word to the sergeant to follow him, he crossed the narrow stretch of rutted road and made his way along the shadow of the high hedge, peering intently into the darkness to discover some means of admittance; but the hedge was thick, and there was no break. Presently, however, it ended abruptly, giving way to a barbed wire fence that enclosed, so far as he could see, a tract of meadowland.

With infinite difficulty, and at the cost of a ripped coat, he succeeded in squeezing his huge bulk between two strands of the wire, muttering to Leek to follow his example.

The lean sergeant had just obeyed, when Mr. Budd gripped his arm, and breathed a warning in his ear.

Away in the distance came the sound of

a car. It grew steadily louder as it approached. Presently they saw the gleam of its headlights as it swung into the narrow lane, and then it passed them, and came to a halt outside the gates of the farm. A muffled figure, whose sex it was impossible to distinguish, got out and tapped softly on the wicket-gate. There was a long pause, and then the little gate was apparently opened by someone inside, for the figure disappeared. Again there was a short silence, broken by the rasping of bolts.

The car was backed a few yards in the direction of the watchers, and then driven forward. As it turned, Mr. Budd saw that the main gates were now wide open. The car passed within, and they heard the low murmur of voices. There was no sound of the gates closing, and the big man concluded that other visitors were expected. His conclusion proved correct, for after the lapse of a few minutes the sound of a footstep became audible coming down the lane. It was a light step, and as it came nearer he caught a glimpse of the walker. It was a woman. She advanced quickly, and, as she passed the place where they crouched in the rank grass, a momentary whiff of perfume was wafted to Mr. Budd's nostrils. It was a familiar perfume — the perfume used by the girl who had come down the stairs at Shepton Manor.

4

The Secret of the Barn

Mr. Budd watched her turn into the open gateway of the farm, and pursed his lips. There was no reason why she should not visit Mr. Osborne, and yet — The stout man shook his head. Was he allowing the chance remarks of a handful of stupidly superstitious villagers to bias his judgment? The most likely explanation of these visitors to Boyle's Farm was that the owner was giving a party. Probably the rooms in the house were small, and he had converted the barn into a lounge or something of the sort, in order to avoid overcrowding his guests. This seemed a perfectly reasonable supposition, but all the same, Mr. Budd was not completely satisfied with it. For one thing, it was a queer time to start a party, especially in a small village like Shepton Magna, and for another, there was something furtive in the way the girl had arrived. No, he was certainly not satisfied that everything was quite open and above board.

The sound of another car approaching broke in on his musings. It came from the opposite direction to the first, slowed when it reached the entrance to the farm, and passed through the gateway. Again came the sound of low, whispering voices, and then the soft laugh of a woman. The deep tones of a man said something, and a woman's voice replied, but Mr. Budd could not catch what was said

The stout superintendent stifled a yawn and settled down to wait further developments. Whether this was just an innocent party to which Mr. Osborne had invited a few friends, or whether it was something more, he intended to see it through.

During the next half-hour a great many people arrived, some on foot, some in cars — Mr. Budd counted seven cars in all — and then the gates were shut, and he heard the bolts shot back into their sockets.

'That's the lot, apparently,' he murmured to the weary Leek. 'If he were expectin' any more he wouldn't have shut the gates.'

'Well, what do we do now?' asked the sergeant. 'The damp's gettin' into me bones. If I don't look out I shall be laid up with an attack of the rheumatics.'

'Well, look out!' grunted the unsympathetic Mr. Budd. 'I never knew such a feller for grumblin' as you. Why don't you try bein' cheerful for a change?'

'I don't see much ter be cheerful at,' replied Leek lugubriously. 'This ain't a very cheerful spot, an' it's gettin' late — '

'It'll get later!' snapped his superior. 'Now stop worryin' about your creature comforts, an' attend to business. I'm goin' to have a look inside that barn by hook or by crook, so let's get goin'!'

'Where to?' inquired the unhappy sergeant, with a sigh.

'Oh, to the Canary Islands!' snarled Mr. Budd irritably. 'Where d'you think? Where would you go if you wanted to see inside that barn?'

'Why, to the barn, o' course!' replied Leek. 'That's obvious, ain't it?'

'It's so obvious,' retorted the big man, 'that I should have thought even you could have seen it without having to ask stupid questions.'

'What I meant was,' explained the long-suffering Leek, in an injured voice, 'how are we goin' ter get there?'

'Well, we can't fly, can we?' growled Mr. Budd, 'so we shall have to walk.'

He moved away across the uneven surface of the meadow towards the hedge that divided it from the land in the immediate vicinity of the farm, and began to explore its length. It grew less thickly than the other, and after a considerable amount of trouble, for it was difficult to see anything in that darkness, and he dared not risk a light, he found what he sought — an opening sufficient to squeeze through. He promptly took advantage of this piece of good luck and found himself within a few yards of the barn.

'Now don't go and fall over anythin',' he whispered in Leek's ear, 'an' try and move about as though you wasn't a herd of maraudin' elephants! I don't want anybody to spot us.'

He began to pick his way cautiously towards the dim building that reared up in front of them. The light still blazed out from the square window in the apex of the roof, but otherwise there was darkness. Not a ray percolated through any chink or cranny in the tarred planks, or showed where the big double doors, tightly closed, formed practically the whole of one end of the building.

Mr. Budd stopped when he reached the side of the barn, and caressed his massive chin thoughtfully. It looked as if he had had all his trouble for nothing. Except the window, which was too high to be accessible without the aid of a ladder, there was no means by which a sight of the interior of the building could be obtained. Pressing his ear to the wall, he listened. A muffled, droning hum of voices reached him, but that was all. It was too vague to convey even the slightest suggestion of what was going on inside, except that there seemed to be a number of people all talking at once.

The big man frowned. He was intensely

curious to know what was taking place in the barn. It was quite likely that it was nothing of any importance, judged, that is, in relation to the inquiry he was undertaking, but it was decidedly queer, and his experience had taught him that queer things were usually worthwhile investigating. Therefore, he cast round in his mind for a means of achieving his object.

So far as he could see, there was only one way, and that was to reach the window through which the light blazed steadily. But although it was easy to reach this conclusion, it was not easy at all to reach the window. It was a good fifteen feet from the ground, and the only way to get to it would be with a ladder. Now was there a ladder anywhere near at hand? Very probably there was — a farm without a ladder was unthinkable — but how was it possible to find such a thing in pitch darkness without a knowledge of the lay of the land? Too see into that barn, however, he was determined.

He confided the problem in a whisper to Leek, and the lean sergeant scratched the side of his head.

'Why not give it up?' he suggested helpfully. 'I don't see 'ow you're goin'ter find a ladder without you know where ter look.'

Mr. Budd suppressed his natural annoyance.

'We can but try,' he said. 'Come on!'

He began to explore among the outbuildings, moving stealthily, and alert for the slightest sound that would warn him of anyone's presence, for if everything was quite innocent he would find it difficult to explain his position if he were discovered prowling about private property at that hour.

After nearly an hour's search, he found a ladder, and the next difficulty was to carry it to the barn without making a noise. With the sergeant's help, he succeeded, and eventually they found themselves back at the point from which they had started, plus the rather unwieldy ladder.

With great care they raised it up on end and set it very gently against the side of the building containing the window. It reached to a few inches below the narrow sill, and Mr. Budd, wiping the perspiration from his forehead with the back of his hand, prepared to ascend.

He mounted carefully while the sergeant held the bottom of the ladder to prevent it slipping. If, by any chance, someone should attempt to leave the barn, nothing could save them from discovery, for the ladder was immediately in front of the entrance. That risk had to be taken, however, since there was no other way of reaching the window.

Slowly, like a rather fat spider, Mr. Budd moved upwards from rung to rung. Presently the watching Leek saw his head silhouetted against the light that streamed out from the window, and he stopped.

At first the stout superintendent could make out nothing. The window was dirty, and all he could see was a hazy glare of light that seemed to be concentrated at the opposite end of the long building. And then gradually, as his eyes became accustomed to the circumstances, he began to distinguish various objects, until the whole picture was clear. And what he saw brought a sudden stoppage to his breath and sent him rigid.

The interior of that barn was like no other barn in the world. The walls were hung with some kind of black material, caught up and festooned from the centre of the roof. The floor was covered with a carpet of the same funereal hue, and set in rows were a number of chairs facing a raised dais on which was an altar. The whole appearance of the place was that of a chapel, but such a chapel as Mr. Budd had never seen before in his life, and never wanted to see again.

Great black candles in huge black sconces flanked the steps that led up to the altar. They flared like torches of old, and the big superintendent could faintly smell the pitch of which they were evidently composed. On the altar itself stood a crucifix, but it was upside down, and before this, clad in the vestments of a priest, a man faced the scattered congregation that occupied the rows of chairs. It was Osborne!

There was no mistaking the little smear of moustache that lay along his upper lip;

no mistaking, either, the meaning of this strange and rather weird assembly. Here, in the heart of the country, the Black Mass was being celebrated! These people gathered together in that converted barn were Devil-worshippers!

5

Through Hell and Back

That queer, cold sensation that he had experienced in the bar of the Shepton Arms once more trickled down Mr. Budd's spine. He had seen many unpleasant things during the course of his long career, but this was horrible! There was something beastly and obscene in that horrid travesty of a chapel; in the fascinated faces of the people watching the ghastly celebration; in the fact that such a disgusting orgy could draw devotees from apparently respectable and intelligent members of society.

The big man shivered. The whole case of the vanishing men now took on a dreadful significance that was nightmarish. Was it something connected with these ancient blasphemous rites that formed the motive for their sudden disappearance? It seemed to the watching superintendent that it was more than possible. The rumours, then, in the district, had not been without foundation. The village people had suspected that there was a revival of Black Magic, and they had been right. Here was Mr. Budd, himself, witnessing one of the chief ceremonies.

He considered what he should do, and came to the conclusion that for the present he would do nothing. It would be wiser to act warily.

He came down from his precarious perch and rejoined the waiting Leek.

'Help me to get this ladder back where we found it,' he whispered a little huskily.

'What was happenin'? What was they doin'?' asked the sergeant eagerly.

'Playin' hopscotch,' answered Mr. Budd. 'Don't talk. Give me a hand with this ladder.'

He eased it gingerly away from the side of the barn, and they carried it back across the yard without mishap.

'Well, fancy goin' to all that trouble jest ter find a lot of silly people playin' hopscotoh,' remarked Leek, when they had crawled back through the gap in the hedge and were once more in the lane outside Boyle's Farm. 'I s'pose we can go back ter bed now?'

'Yes,' said Mr. Budd soberly. 'I think that's the best thing we can do.'

★ ★ ★

Mr. Budd woke early on the following morning in spite of a disturbed night, for his sleep had been broken by unpleasant dreams. For some time he lay staring up at the ceiling of his bedroom as wakefulness brought back memory, and he recalled the events of the night. Then he got up, pulled on his shabby dressing gown, and went over to the window.

It was a grey, drear morning, and the outlook was depressing.

The big man yawned, and consulting his watch, found that it was barely five. He sat down on the edge of his bed, reached for his waistcoat, and found one of his thin, black cigars. This he stuck between his teeth, but although there were matches on the small table near the bed, he didn't light it.

The sight he had witnessed in that barn at Boyle's Farm was still vivid in his mind. It had shaken him severely, and he had not yet got over the emotion it had aroused. It was a curious emotion, a compound of fear and disgust, and he had experienced it only once before in his life. During a visit to the reptile house at the zoo.

Sitting there in the cold light of early morning, chewing on the end of his unlighted cigar, he decided that he didn't like it at all. It was a nasty business; a business that involved all sorts of queer kinks and mental disorders; more the business of a doctor than a detective. And that girl — what was her name? Linley, that was it — she had been present at that beastly orgy, and so had the nephew, Arthur Grenton. He had recognised him among that depraved assembly. A nasty business without a doubt. Young Kilfoyle had been one of the men who had vanished. Had he been spirited away because he had found out what was going on, or for some other and more sinister reason? The stout man had only the very vaguest knowledge of the rites of Devil-worship — a smattering garnered from something he had once read — but he seemed to remember that there was a mention of human sacrifice.

Surely that couldn't be at the back of these disappearances? It hadn't been, anyway, in the case of poor Tom Hardiman. The sacrificial victims, from what he remembered, usually died by the knife. Blood had to be shed.

But Hardiman might very easily have discovered something and been silenced because of what he knew. Only that didn't account for the lapse of time between his disappearance and his death. Where had he been during that period — at Boyle's Farm? If so, was that where the others were?

At this point the stout superintendent pulled himself up. He was taking it for granted that what he had witnessed the previous night — or rather in the very early hours of that morning — had a bearing on the case he had come to investigate, and there was no direct evidence of this. The fact that Devil-worship had been revived in the district might have nothing to do with the vanishing men. There was no tangible connection whatsoever. He must be careful to guard against jumping to conclusions.

The light outside grew steadily stronger, and there came the sound of movements from somewhere below, but still he sat on, a frown distorting his heavy face, oblivious to everything but his thoughts.

Presently a sleepy-eyed servant brought his tea, and he roused himself with a yawn, stretching stiffly.

While he dressed he made his plans for the day, quite unaware that none of them would be put into practice. For the morning was to bring a development that changed his whole outlook, and, incidentally, provided him with a clue that was eventually to lead him to the truth.

He was having breakfast with the lugubrious Leek when Inspector Mumble arrived, almost bursting with excitement.

'Young Mr. Kilfoyle's come back!' he announced breathlessly. 'Sir David telephoned to the station a quarter of an hour ago — '

'Come back, has he?' broke in Mr. Budd, swallowing a large mouthful of toast and marmalade very suddenly. 'H'm! Now, that's interestin' and peculiar. Where does he say he's been?'

'I 'aven't seen 'im yet,' replied Mumble. 'I thought I'd come and let you know what had happened on my way up to the manor.'

'Now that's what I call very thoughtful, very thoughtful indeed,' remarked the big man. He gulped down a full cup of tea, and rose ponderously to his feet. 'I think I'll come along with you and hear what this young man has to say for himself.'

'Just 'alf a second,' put in Leek, making a desperate effort to talk and eat at the same time, 'an' I'll be with you.'

'There's no need for you to be with us',' said Mr. Budd. 'An' don't talk with your mouth full!'

In his indignation the lean sergeant allowed a piece of toast to slip down the wrong way, and before he had recovered from the fit of coughing it induced, Mr. Budd and the inspector had gone.

Mumble's dilapidated car was drawn

up outside the inn, and if it did not exactly speed them to Shepton Manor, it was at least quicker than walking, and less tiring.

They were admitted by the servant whom Mr. Budd had seen on his previous visit, and conducted at once to the library.

Sir David Kilfoyle was standing before the great mantelpiece, but this time he was alone. There was no sign of Grenton, and the fat detective wondered whether he was still sleeping off the effects of his night's entertainment. The bald-headed man greeted them pleasantly, and there was no trace of the strained anxiety that had been on his face before.

'This is a happier occasion than our last meeting,' he said genially, smiling at Mr. Budd. 'As the inspector, here, has no doubt told you, my son has returned.'

'So I understand, sir,' murmured the big man, nodding. 'I'm very glad to hear it, very glad indeed. When did he come back?'

'Early this morning,' replied Sir David. 'In fact, a few minutes before I telephoned to Inspector Mumble. He was in a very weak state and I insisted that he should go straight to bed.'

'Did he explain the reason for his absence?' asked Mr. Budd.

Sir David shook his head.

'I didn't question him,' he answered. 'What he wanted was food and rest. I thought it better to leave hearing his story until you arrived, and so avoid his having to tell it twice. I must admit, however, that I'm very curious and since, by now, he will have finished the meal that was sent up to him, we will go and hear what he has to say, if you are agreeable.'

Mr. Budd was more than agreeable. He was intensely interested to hear the story, although outwardly he still looked his rather bored and weary self.

Sir David led the way up the huge staircase, down a long corridor, and stopped at a closed door on the right.

'Can I come in, Alec?' he called, and a voice from inside replied in the affirmative. Pushing open the door the old man ushered them into a large room and introduced the stout superintendent to a pale-faced, youngish-looking man who lay propped up with pillows in the big bed.

Alec Kilfoyle looked ill and tired. There were dark circles round his eyes, and his straw-coloured hair was long, although some attempt had been made to brush it into a semblance of neatness. From the smoothness of his chin Mr. Budd judged that he had recently shaved, and discovered, later, that this was true. When he had arrived at Shepton Manor he had been the possessor of a straggling growth of beard.

'How are you feeling now?' asked Sir David, eyeing his son sympathetically.

'Heaps better,' was the reply. 'That breakfast old Batson brought up has put new life into me. All I want now is a long sleep and I shall be as well as ever.'

'You're sure you wouldn't like a doctor — ' began his father, but the young man shook his head.

'No, no,' he declared. 'All I want is food and rest — and lots of it. I got precious little of either in that horrible place.' He gave a sudden shiver and pulled at the cigarette he was smoking, jerkily.

'We'd like to hear about that, sir,' said Mr. Budd, rubbing his chin gently. 'What happened to you on the twenty-seventh of March, and where have you been since?'

Alec Kilfoyle blew a cloud of smoke from between his lips, and looked at him through it.

'I've been through hell and back!' he said seriously, and began one of the strangest stories that the stout man had ever listened to.

6

The One Who Came Back

'It happened on my return from Marley Halt,' began Alec Kilfoyle. 'I'd been, as you know, to fetch a parcel from the station, and I was returning home when, just by Boyle's Farm, the back tyre punctured. I was annoyed at the accident because it meant being late for dinner, and I was hungry. I'd just got down to set about changing the wheel when a man appeared. I don't know where he came from; one minute he wasn't there, and the next he was. He seemed more or less to have materialised from nowhere, if you understand what I mean. Probably I had been too busy examining the damage to the tyre to notice his approach until he was beside me.

'Anyway, it gave me quite a little shock to find him suddenly there. He was a complete stranger to me — a big, bearded fellow, rather shabbily dressed, and wearing a cap pulled down over his eyes — not a nice-looking customer by any means. He asked me what the matter was, and I told him, noticing that there was a queer, pungent smell about him that seemed vaguely familiar. He muttered something that I did not catch, and then without warning he suddenly flung himself on me and forced a reeking pad over my mouth and nose. I knew then what the stuff was I had smelt. It was chloroform!

'I struggled as hard as I could, but he was abnormally strong, and I might have been a child for all the good my struggles did. In spite of the fact that I tried to hold my breath the drug got into my lungs, and after a short while I felt my senses reeling. I redoubled my efforts to break free from his grip, and then everything went black, and I don't remember anything more until I came to myself and found that I was somewhere in pitch darkness and securely bound, hand and foot.'

He paused, inhaled a lungful of smoke,

and let it trickle slowly through his nostrils.

'I had no idea where I was,' he went on, 'or the reason for the attack that had been made on me. I don't even know that now. As well as being bound, I had been gagged, and the after-effects of the chloroform had left me with a splitting headache and an unpleasant feeling of sickness. It was a long time before I realised that there was anyone else in the place with me, but eventually I heard breathing, and guessed that I was not alone. And then it suddenly struck me that the same thing that had happened to Tom Hardiman and Hickthorne had happened to me.

'They had suddenly disappeared, and now, of course, I had done the same. It was not a nice situation, and I began to wonder what was behind it all, and who was responsible.

'The place to which I had been brought was very quiet. There wasn't a sound anywhere except the heavy breathing near me, and a curious lapping noise that was like water. I found out much later that it was water, and that I had been taken on board a boat, but I'll come to that presently.

'After a long time — it seemed like years to me — the man who had attacked me came in with a candle and gave me food and water. He had to remove the gag to allow me to eat, and I demanded to know what the idea was, but he wouldn't even answer. As soon as I'd eaten the bread and drunk the water he put the gag on again and went over and did the same with my two companions whom I was able to recognise as Hardiman and the doctor. Then he went out, without having opened his mouth to speak once.

'This went on day after day until I had lost count of time. And then, during one visit, he took Hardiman away. I don't know what happened to him, but I never saw him again.'

'I can tell you what happened to him, poor feller,' broke in Mr. Budd soberly. 'He was found dead in the pond by Boyle's Farm.'

Alec Kilfoyle stared at him in horror
'Good God!' he muttered. 'How

dreadful! What's the reason for this ghastly business?'

'Maybe we'll get at that after you've finished your story, sir,' said the big man hopefully.

Young Kilfoyle shook his head

'I don't think it will help you much,' he replied. 'However I'll go on. Just after Hardiman was taken away another prisoner arrived, young Pilcher, the boy at the vicarage. The same routine was carried out as before. Once every day we were fed on a hunk of bread and given a glass of water, for the rest of the time we lay helpless in the dark, unable to speak because of the gags, and unable to reach each other because of the rope which fastened us to the walls of the cabin as well as binding our feet and ankles.

'As I've said, I had lost all count of time. There was no difference in the darkness in which we were kept between night and day, and the only break was when our captor came to feed us. And now I am coming to the crowning horror of that horrible period.'

Once again he paused to draw in

smoke deeply from his cigarette and crush out the end in an ashtray on the table at his side.

'I shall always remember it.' he continued, 'even if I live to be a hundred. It was ghastly, horrible, a nightmare! I saw Hickthorne and Pilcher killed before my eyes.'

He stopped abruptly, and moistened his lips, and something of the horror that he had felt communicated itself to his audience.

'That bearded monster did it!' he said. 'He came in and killed them both — stabbed them — and when he had made sure that both were dead, he turned to me with the most horrible grin I've ever seen on any human face. 'I'm going now,' he said. 'And I shan't be coming back. You can starve, and I hope you like it! You'll have good company, anyhow.' And then he left me — alone in the dark with those dead men.'

'Alec!' There was horror and disgust in Sir David's exclamation. 'Good heavens, how dreadful! What a terrible thing to do! The man must have been mad.'

'I think he was,' said Alec Kilfoyle, 'though he didn't look it. I can't think of any other explanation for it all. And I think I must have gone a little mad after that. I remember very little of what happened during the rest of the time I was a prisoner in that beastly place with those two poor fellows, or rather what was left of them. I believe I shouted and screamed without realising that the gag choked back all sound, and I know that I tugged and strained at the ropes that bound me until I was completely exhausted. I never want to go through a time like that again. It was hellish! I must have been locked up without food for several days, locked up with two dead men in a tiny space that was no bigger than a large tool-shed.'

'How did you succeed in escaping?' asked Mr. Budd.

'My constant struggles must have loosened the ropes,' replied Kilfoyle, 'for, during last night, to my intense joy, I suddenly found myself free. It was a long time, however, before I could move. The lack of food, and having to lie still for so long, had left me as weak as a rat. I managed at last to struggle to my feet and stagger over to the door of the cabin. It was locked, of course, but I found an old box and was able to smash it open. I hauled myself up the ladder outside and found I was on the deck of an old sloop that was moored to the bank of the river.'

'Which river, sir?' interrupted Mumble, speaking for the first time.

'The Marl,' answered Kilfoyle. 'It was moored in one of those lonely reaches up by Loxham, you know where I mean?'

'Yes, I know, sir,' said the inspector, nodding.

'Well,' remarked Mr. Budd, pulling gently at his nose, 'you seem to have had a very unpleasant experience, sir. But it's a good thing it was no worse. I s'pose you'd know this bearded feller again, if you was to see him?'

'I certainly should,' declared Kilfoyle emphatically. 'I hope you can find him.'

'I hope so, too, sir,' said the big man. 'I s'pose it never struck you that he was disguised?'

'No, it didn't,' was the reply, 'and I

don't think he was. If he was, it was a very clever disguise.'

'What on earth could his object have been?' muttered Sir David, frowning. 'Why should he have wanted to kill these people? It was the act of a madman.'

'I'm sure he was as crazy as a coot,' said his son. 'He must have been. There's no other explanation.'

'Well, sir,' said Mr. Budd. 'I'm very glad you got away. He might have killed you, too, when the others had been stabbed, instead of leaving you to starve.' He yawned and blinked sleepily. 'I think we'd better be goin' along to this boat and see if we can't find somethin'. How far is it?'

'About ten miles from here,' said Inspector Mumble. 'In a wild bit o' country where the river runs through marshes. That's where you mean, isn't it, sir?'

Young Kilfoyle nodded.

'That's right,' he said, and added with a weary smile: 'And now I'm going to sleep. I'm so tired I can scarcely keep my eyes open.'

They left him and returned downstairs. There they took their leave of the relieved Sir David, and went back to Mumble's decrepit car.

'Well, this is a queer affair, isn't it?' said the inspector as he tried with difficulty to start the engine.

'It certainly is,' grunted Mr. Budd. 'I s'pose it was a car once, though.'

Mumble looked hurt.

'I was talkin' about wot we've just 'eard,' he protested. 'This car's all right. Once it starts it goes like a house on fire.'

'Just like,' agreed the fat detective, and went on: 'Yes, as you say, it's a queer business.'

The obstinate engine started at that moment with a noise like a miniature air raid, and they shot down the drive. In Inspector Mumble's car it was impossible to hold a conversation while the machine was moving. Shout as you might, your voice would not rise above the clatter of the engine and the rattle of the various loose pieces of which it was composed. Mr. Budd, therefore, closed his eyes and gave himself up to his thoughts.

It took them nearly an hour and a half to reach their objective, and the surrounding country grew wilder and less inviting as they proceeded. Presently they came in sight of the moored sloop, half aground amid a tangle of rushes. It was a dilapidated old boat, and looked on the verge of falling to pieces. Mr. Budd eyed it disparagingly when Mumble brought the car to a coughing halt.

'Who does it belong to?' he asked.

'Don't know,' answered the inspector, getting out. 'It's been there for years. Shouldn't think it belonged to anyone.'

They approached the wreck and sought for a means of climbing on board. But there was nothing but an ancient piece of rope that dangled from the stern.

The stout man grunted when the inspector suggested that they should climb up this.

'I'm not built for swarming up ropes,' he said, shaking his head. 'You might be able to manage it, but I couldn't.'

Mumble eventually did manage it, and surveyed his companion from the deck.

'You look just like Nelson,' said Mr.

Budd, 'or the feller that discovered America. Now how am I goin' to get up there?'

This problem was solved by the discovery of a ladder that was provided with hooks, and was evidently intended for the purpose of boarding the craft. The fat man negotiated it with difficulty, but without mishap, and joined the inspector on the deck.

Descending the narrow companion-way they came to the shattered door of the cabin, and pushed it open. Inside it was dark, for the portholes and the glazed hatch had been covered with tarpaulin. Mr. Budd had a torch with him, however, and, switching this on, he sent the light zigzagging about the small saloon. It rested at last on the floor, and on two dark objects that lay there.

'You know Hickthorne and Pilcher,' muttered the stout superintendent. 'Have a look, and tell me if they are them.'

Reluctantly the inspector went over and peered down gingerly at the two bodies.

'It's them right enough,' he reported, and stumbled hastily back to the door. 'I think we'd better get that hatch open before we do anything further. It's not very healthy in there. They've been dead a good while, I should say.'

'I should say so, too,' agreed Mr. Budd. 'Let's get busy.'

7

The Mob

When the atmosphere had cleared a little, Mr. Budd and the inspector made a careful search of the old sloop. It was an ancient tub, almost paintless, with rotting timbers, and fittings that had tarnished to a greenish-black. In the galley they found the remains of a loaf of bread, and a barrel of water. The water was brackish; the bread stone hard. Of clues to the identity of the bearded man there was none.

Stifling a natural repugnance, Mr. Budd went back to the saloon and examined the two bodies. Both had been stabbed in the breast, but there was no sign of the weapon used, and both were securely bound and gagged. There was nothing at all in any of the pockets; but under one of the rotting bunks the big man found a black bag containing surgical instruments and other paraphernalia associated with the profession of a doctor. Inspector Mumble took charge of this as an exhibit at the inquest.

Over in a corner they found the gag and the ropes that had been used on Alec Kilfoyle. Mr. Budd made a careful inspection of these, paying particular attention to the knots, and then stowed them away in one of his capacious pockets.

'And that's all,' he grunted, looking round sleepily. 'I don't think we can do much here. One of us had better stay while the other goes and fetches a doctor an' an ambulance.'

'I'll stay,' volunteered the inspector, which was exactly what the big man had hoped for. 'You can take my car.'

'It 'ud be quicker to walk,' said Mr. Budd, but he took the car all the same.

When he had notified the discovery at the police station and seen the ambulance depart with the doctor, accompanied by a sergeant and two constables, he rejoined Leek at the inn.

The lean sergeant was full of curiosity to hear what Alec Kilfoyle had had to say, and when Mr. Budd told him he scratched his head.

'It makes it all the more puzzlin', don't it?' he remarked. 'Who could this feller with the beard 'ave bin, an' what in the world did he want ter do it for?'

'I'd like to know what he did it for,' murmured Mr. Budd thoughtfully. 'As to who he is — well, I could, I think, give a very good guess.'

Leek stared at him in astonishment.

'You don't mean ter say you know 'im?' he gasped.

'I don't mean to say so, and I didn't say so,' snapped the stout superintendent, irritably. 'I said I thought I could guess.'

'Well, who d'you think it is, then?' demanded the sergeant.

'I'll tell you when it's more than thinkin',' said Mr. Budd. 'It's the 'why' that's worrying me. I can't figure that out at all.'

'I can't figure any of it out,' said Leek candidly

'Well go away in a corner an' keep quiet,' grunted Mr. Budd. 'I want to put in some heavy brain work.'

He spent the rest of the afternoon lying on his bed, smoking innumerable black cigars, and staring at the ceiling.

At five o'clock Leek appeared to inform him that the chief constable wanted to see him. Mr. Budd scowled at the disturber of his thoughts, but hoisted himself ponderously off the bed.

'Where is he?' he demanded, splashing water into the basin.

'Downstairs in the sittin' room,' answered the sergeant.

The stout superintendent laved his face, washed his hands, and descended the stairs.

Colonel Wrayford was waiting impatiently in the little back room.

'I've just heard the news,' he said abruptly 'I was away on business all day, and I've only just received Mumble's report. What do you think of this latest development, eh?'

'I haven't come to any definite conclusion, sir,' said Mr. Budd, suppressing a yawn.

The chief constable looked a little irritable

'It seems to me that this man Kilfoyle speaks about — this fellow with the beard — must be a lunatic,' he declared. 'That's the only conclusion I can come to. Don't you agree?'

'I don't know that I do altogether, sir,' said the stout man, pulling gently at his nose and looking sleepily at the other.

'Then what do you suggest his motive can have been?' demanded Colonel Wrayford.

'I can't suggest anything, sir,' murmured Mr. Budd, shaking his head.

The chief constable suppressed an angry exclamation. Good gad, were all Scotland Yard detectives like this bovine, sleepy-eyed man before him? If so, no wonder there were so many unsolved crimes. This fellow didn't look as if he could find a lost collar stud, and he had been told that he was the cleverest of them all.

'Well,' he said sharply, 'this man will have to be found. He's killed three people, and, whether he is a lunatic or not, he's a danger while he is at large.'

'I quite agree with you, sir,' said Mr.

Budd, 'an' I don't think you need worry. I'll find him, though maybe he won't be wearin' his beard.'

'You mean you think he was disguised?' asked Wrayford.

'No, sir, I didn't mean that at all,' corrected the big man. 'I don't think he was disguised.'

'I wish,' said the chief constable crossly, 'that you would say, plainly, what you do mean.'

'I couldn't say what I mean plainly, sir,' replied Mr. Budd sadly, 'because I don't really know what I do mean. I've got a vague idea, as you might say. Like a picture that's been taken out of focus. I can guess the 'who' but I can't guess the 'why', if you understand me? It's that that's beatin' me — the 'why'.'

Colonel Wrayford stared at him.

'Are you seriously stating that you know the identity of this man?' he said in astonishment.

'Yes, sir, I think I do,' answered Mr. Budd simply.

'Then he must be arrested at once!' declared the chief constable, but Mr.

Budd shook his head.

'No, sir, if you'll excuse me contradicting you,' he said. 'There's not enough evidence to justify his arrest.'

'Not enough evidence!' echoed the colonel. 'But good heavens, man, we've got the evidence of Alec Kilfoyle! He saw two of the murders committed! If you can find the man, he can identify him. You can't have any better evidence than an eye-witness.'

'I don't think that Mr. Kilfoyle would be able to identify the man, sir,' murmured Mr. Budd. 'In fact, if I'm right, I'm sure he wouldn't. I can't explain any more, sir, but I'd be glad if you'd let me handle this in me own way.'

The chief constable frowned. He disliked this talking in riddles. If this fat, lethargic man knew anything, why didn't he say straight out what he knew?

In the colonel's opinion, what he had said was all nonsense. He was just trying to be mysterious because he didn't know any more than anybody else who the unknown man was who had abducted Kilfoyle and killed the others. He was completely at sea, and was merely trying to save his reputation. What he wanted was time to try to get hold of something, only he didn't want to say so in so many words. Well, if that was the case, it would do no harm to let him have his own way.

'Very well, Superintendent,' he said, a little coldly. 'I won't interfere with your methods, but I shall expect results.'

'Thank you, sir,' said Mr. Budd, knowing perfectly well what had been passing through the other's mind. 'I think that I can promise you results.'

And at that the interview ended.

When the chief constable had driven away, Mr. Budd also left the inn, and strolled in the direction of the tiny police station. Inspector Mumble was not there, and the big man was rather glad than otherwise. He asked the sergeant in charge if he might use the little office, received a ready permission, and shut himself in with the telephone. He put through several calls, concluding with a long conversation with Scotland Yard.

Dusk was falling when he came out and started to walk ponderously back to the

Shepton Arms. He passed several groups of villagers on his way, all whispering together animatedly, and eyed them curiously. They stopped abruptly as he drew near and remained silent until he had passed. Something was up, he thought, and wondered what.

When he reached the inn the only occupant of the bar was Leek. The lean sergeant was sitting mournfully on a settle, and he hailed the advent of his superior with a sigh of relief.

'Where's everybody this evenin'?' demanded Mr. Budd, looking round the deserted bar with raised brows.

Leek shook his narrow head.

'Queer, ain't it?' he said. 'There ain't been a soul in 'ere ternight. Must be somethin' on.'

Mr. Budd went up to the bar and rapped sharply with half-a-crown.

'Pint o' bitter, please,' he said, when the landlord appeared, and while the man was drawing the beer: 'Where's all the customers?'

'There's a meeting on,' replied the landlord. 'Maybe they'll be in presently.'

But he was wrong, for nobody came into the Shepton Arms during the whole of the evening. The stout superintendent was puzzled. Something peculiar was brewing, but what?

The question was answered unexpectedly but dramatically.

Mr. Budd and the sergeant were in the middle of supper when the big man paused with his fork half-way to his mouth.

'What's the matter?' asked Leek.

'Listen!' snapped Mr. Budd. 'D'you hear that?'

From outside, vaguely audible, came a faint, continuous sound, like the murmur of waves on a distant beach.

'Yes, what is it?' said the sergeant.

Without answering, Mr. Budd got up and went over to the small casement window. Opening it, he leaned out, staring at the sight that met his gaze.

The village green was thick with people. The entire population seemed to have gathered in one mass, and, even as he looked, belated stragglers were hurrying to join the dense throng. The moon was out and he could see the strange scene clearly. At the cottage doors near by, women were standing, talking to their neighbours excitedly, and there was an unmistakable angry note to the dull chorus of voices.

'I don't like the look o' things,' said Mr. Budd seriously. 'There's going to be trouble, I'm afraid.'

'What d'yer mean — ' began Leek, but the stout superintendent was already making for the door.

As they came out into the night the sound of the voices swelled to a roar, and now they could see that the multitude was being addressed by the sweep, who stood in the midst of the seething throng upon some kind of improvised rostrum. More ominous still, Mr. Budd saw that every one of that excited mob was armed with stakes and farm implements. There were pitchforks and spades, hoes and sickles, and in one or two cases, axes. When they got near to the fringe of the crowd they caught what the hoarse voice of the sweep was saying.

' . . . stop it for good an' all. We ain't

goin' ter stand fer no more of it. 'E was at 'is devil-work an' witchcraft last night agin. Wasn't that there light a-burnin' in the barn until the sun rose? An' this mornin' Mrs. Kelvin's kid is took ill an' dies. The doctor says as how she'd bin eating poisoned berries, but do we believe that, mates? Does any of you believe that? No! We knows what killed the kid, we knows what killed old Belton an' put the blight on Fenlock's crops, we knows why the doctor an' poor Tom 'Ardiman an' George Pilcher an' young Mr. Kilfoyle vanished like wot they did, an' we ain't goin' to stand fer no more of it.'

'To Boyle's Farm! To Boyle's Farm!' The angry cry, roared from a hundred throats, drowned the rest of the sweep's speech, and he disappeared in the middle of the surging throng as it moved forward.

'To the farm! To the farm!' The cry was taken up and tossed from mouth to mouth until the night rang with it.

'Burn it! Burn it to the ground!' screamed a voice, and it was answered by a roar of approval. Seldom had Mr. Budd seen a mob in such an ugly, dangerous mood. A blaze of light sprang up somewhere, followed by another and another as pitch-soaked rags, wrapped round tree branches, were lighted and waved aloft. The lurid, smoky glare of these hastily made torches lit up the grim faces of the crowd as they began to march in a straggling procession towards Boyle's Farm.

Large numbers of women, shouting encouragement, kept pace with the uneven column, and the babble of tongues swelled to a deafening volume. From cottages, from side lanes, from everywhere, other men and women came hurrying to join the main throng, and in the rear went Mr. Budd and the startled Leek, helpless to stem that maddened mob, but hoping against hope that something might yet be done to prevent the danger that threatened.

The mob went sweeping on its way, gathering fresh energy as it moved towards its objective, and momentarily becoming more imbued with that half-hysterical excitement that is one of the peculiarities of mass psychology. The majority of the people were good honest working men — farm labourers and cowhands — who had worked themselves into a passion over what they considered was a righteous cause. But there was another element, too.

Every town and every village has its black sheep, and Mr. Budd was able to pick out several among the throng. These hooligans cared little for the reason for the demonstration. All that they were after was the excitement. It was easy to tell them. They were making the most noise, and their threatening shouts were wilder. They had worked their way up to a position in the van of the procession, and were urging the rest onward, keeping the emotions of the crowd at fever heat.

'Ain't there nothin' we can do?' muttered Leek uneasily. 'There'll be murder done if we ain't careful.'

'I know,' said Mr. Budd, with a worried frown, 'but we can't do anythin' at the moment. It 'ud be hopeless to try to stop 'em.'

At that moment he saw a cyclist patrol

coming towards them. The policeman stared at the approaching crowd that filled the narrow roadway, and dismounted.

''Ere,' he demanded, 'what's the game, eh? What's all this?'

He was swept aside like a leaf before a gale of wind.

'Don't you go tryin' to interfere, Rogers,' shouted a voice. 'We're goin' up to the farm, an' no one ain't goin' ter to stop us!'

'Ay, that's right! Come on, come on! Let's find Osborne!' shouted the sweep, who had constituted himself the leader.

'And lynch 'im!' cried somebody. The cry was taken up.

'Lynch 'im! Lynch 'im!' screamed the mob wrathfully. 'Burn down the farm and lynch Osborne!'

They hurried on, yelling and shrieking, past the helpless constable, and with them, now, went murder.

Mr. Budd paused by the astonished man and touched him on the arm.

'Ride as hard as you can to the station,' he said, 'an' telephone the chief constable. Tell 'im to turn out all the reserves,

214

an' send as many men as 'e can to Boyle's Farm.'

The policeman looked at him dazedly.

'What's happenin', sir?' he began.

'Arson an' murder 'ull be happenin' if you don't do as I tell you!' snapped the big man. 'Don't ask questions. Get a move on!'

The constable touched his helmet, and mounting his bicycle, pedalled off for all he was worth. 'An' that's all we can do,' muttered Mr. Budd. 'Come on. Let's catch up with this crazy lot of idiots.'

The rioters had made good progress, even during the short time it had taken them to speak to the constable. Goaded and excited by the ringleaders, their one desire was to reach their objective and exact vengeance on the man whom they believed was responsible for the various disasters that had happened in the district. The volcano that had been smouldering for months had at last burst into eruption.

At length they reached Boyle's Farm, clustering in a menacing mass round the gates, and now Mr. Budd decided that it was time he took a hand in the proceedings. Somehow or other these maddened people must be stopped doing anything drastic until Colonel Wrayford had time to arrive with sufficient men to disperse them. The fat man forced his way through the yelling multitude until he reached the gates, and there he faced them.

'Stop a moment!' he cried, shouting his loudest to make himself heard above the din. 'Stop a moment I say!'

His appearance was so unexpected that for a moment they did stop. The shouting and the screaming died down to a dull murmur, and he took advantage of the lull.

'You're goin' to do somethin' you'll be sorry for,' he said. 'If you break the law you'll get in trouble — '

'We're the law ternight!' cried the sweep. 'Ye'd best not interfere with us, mister. We've no quarrel with you, but we means ter 'ave our own way. Ain't that right, mates?'

'Ay, that's right, Jim. Out of the way, mister, or you'll be gettin' hurt!'

A big, powerful farmhand, carrying a huge stake advanced threateningly.

'If you're sensible you'll listen to reason!' shouted Mr. Budd, standing his ground. 'Don't you understand that I'm only talkin' to you for your own good? If you don't behave yourselves you'll all land in gaol, an' that won't do any good. Take my advice an' go back to your homes. If this man Osborne has done anything wrong, the law will punish him.'

''E ain't a man, 'e's a devil!' shouted the sweep. 'An we're goin' to put a stop to 'is games once and for all.'

'Out of the way, mister!' roared the big farmhand, and jabbed the heavy stake at Mr. Budd's stomach. It was only a light thrust, but it doubled the stout man up. He staggered back with his hands clasping his capacious middle, completely winded, and the mob, brushing him aside, began a violent assault on the gates.

Leek came hurriedly to his superior's assistance and hauled him out of the way.

'Are you 'urt?' he demanded anxiously.

Mr. Budd grunted. 'What d'yer think?' he gasped, with difficulty. 'How would you like to have a blasted scaffold-pole pushed into your stomach?' He supported himself against a convenient tree and glowered at the frenzied mass of people. 'The fools!' he growled. 'The blithering, brainless fools! Why the heck couldn't they listen to reason?'

But the crowd was beyond reason. The lust for destruction had them in its grip, and they were blind and deaf and dumb to everything except the thing that they had promised themselves.

The gates of the farm were strong, and they withstood the attack well, but the axes which were brought into play prevailed at length, and there was a roar from the throng as the gates finally gave way. They went streaming through, the flickering torches dancing weirdly, and Mr. Budd watched the scene with a sinking heart. It was impossible that the police could arrive in time to prevent them wreaking their vengeance on the property. The only hope was that they would be in time to stop anything more serious.

The noise was terrific. A pandemonium

of shouts and screams and curses. A lurid tongue of flame shot up from the direction of the barn, and was greeted with a yell of delight. It died down, sprang up again, and was followed by an ominous, cracking sound. A thin cloud of smoke mounted steadily to the moonlit sky, increasing in volume as the fire took hold.

In an incredibly short time the barn was blazing from floor to roof, a gigantic bonfire that lit up the surrounding country, and threw into startling relief the figures that darted hither and thither about it. One of the outbuildings burst into flames and added more light to the scene of destruction.

With the countless moving figures, rendered grotesque and unreal by the dancing flames; the billows of smoke and the changing, distorted shadows, it was like hell let loose. For a moment Mr. Budd wondered whether in some extraordinary way the horrible rites that had been enacted in that place had not, after all, succeeded in calling up the devil himself. The drifting smoke had taken on a peculiar form, and with a very little imagination could be likened to a huge figure with a horned head brooding over the farm . . .

The sound of an approaching car checked his fantastic thoughts, and he turned towards the direction from which it came. In a little while the lights of the headlamps showed away up the lane. Was it the police? The car drew nearer, came into the red glare of the burning barn, and stopped. Mr. Budd caught his breath as he recognised it. It was Osborne's!

He knew now why the farm had been in darkness and why there had been no sign of the owner. Osborne had been out, and he had only just returned.

Some of the mob had heard the car, and as Osborne got out a shout went up.

'There 'e is! There's Osborne 'isself!'

A party of thirty or forty men came pouring through the shattered gates, and the owner of the farm was surrounded.

'Come on, lynch 'im!' roared a voice. 'String 'im up to one of 'is own trees!'

'That's right, string 'im up!' The chorus

went up to the lurid night in a howl of delight. 'String 'im up!'

'What does this mean? Let me go, damn you — ' Osborne's voice came faintly through the din, to be drowned by the shouts of the mob.

'We've got ter do somethin'!' muttered Mr. Budd. 'We can't stand by an' see murder done.'

He hurried over to the seething mass of men round the car.

'Let that man alone!' he shouted. 'Let 'im alone! Don't any of you realise that what you're goin' to do is murder? Isn't there a sane man among you? Do you want to hang, you fools?'

'We're goin' ter hang Osborne!' cried a thickset youth, brandishing a pitchfork. 'Out o' the way.'

'If you hang Osborne it's murder, an' you'll suffer for it,' retorted the stout man. 'I'm warnin' you. The police are already on their way here. You've done enough damage. Be content with that. I'm talkin' to you fer your own good.'

One or two of the older and more sober rioters seemed inclined to listen to him, but the others, mad with the fever of destruction, were not going to be done out of their greatest thrill.

'Don't listen to 'im!' shouted the sweep. 'They can't hang all of us. Shove 'im out of the way an' let's get on with the job!'

Half a dozen men seized Mr. Budd, and in spite of his struggles, hauled him away. Leek, alarmed at the turn things were taking, attempted to rescue the big man, but somebody grabbed his hard derby hat and pulled it down over his eyes, where it jammed, effectually blinding him, and resisting all his efforts to remove it.

Mr. Budd, helpless in the grip of three strong farmhands, swore loudly as he watched the terrified, screaming Osborne dragged into the farmyard.

'You'll all pay heavily for this night's work!' he panted. 'If you had one ounce of brains between you, you'd listen to me.'

'You keep quiet,' was the only answer he received.

The farm building was now alight, to

add to the general conflagration, and the leaping flames lit up everything with almost the clearness of noonday. He could see Osborne struggling between a group of men, and others were trying to fling a long rope over the branches of a tall tree. They succeeded as he watched, and a noose was made at the end. He heard the shrieking supplications of Osborne as the loop was passed over his neck. Two big labourers hauled on the slack end, and the kicking man was swung off his feet. For a second he dangled like a giant pendulum, and then —

The throb of engines sounded above the roar of the fire and the shouting of the mob. They swelled louder, and a half a dozen cars came tearing round the bend in the lane, and drew up with squealing brakes in front of the blazing farm.

'Look out!' A warning cry rose from the throats of the crowd, and the swinging body of Osborne fell to the ground as the startled men who were pulling on the rope let go.

Men in uniform and plain clothes tumbled out of the police cars, and among them Mr. Budd recognised Colonel Wrayford.

It was soon over after that. At the sight of the police the less hot-headed gave in at once, and the few who tried to put up a fight were quickly overpowered. An hour after the arrival of the police the mob was routed, but the farm was doomed. Although the fire brigade, which put in an appearance later, did their best, the flames had got too big a hold.

'Nothin' can save that,' remarked Mr. Budd to the chief constable, as they stood watching the holocaust. 'It'll burn to a cinder.'

'Can anybody get this thing off me?' wailed a muffled voice pathetically, and, looking round, Mr. Budd saw the unfortunate Leek, still completely obscured in his hat.

'I forgot all about you,' grunted the big man. 'Come 'ere and let me see what I can do.'

But his efforts were in vain. Although he nearly tore off the sergeant's rather prominent ears, the hat remained tightly wedged.

'You'll have to wait till we get back to the inn an' 'ave it cut off,' said Mr. Budd. 'Though if I was you I'd always wear it like that. It's a great improvement.'

8

Mr. Budd Gets His Man

The fire blazed throughout the night and far into the next day. When at last it burned itself out there was nothing left of Boyle's Farm but a heap of smouldering ruins. Although Osborne had been saved from the fate which the mob had planned for him, the night did not pass without tragedy, for the shock brought on a collapse, and he died while he was being taken to the cottage hospital. His heart had failed.

Mr. Budd got back to the Shepton Arms in the early hours of the morning, and when Leek had been operated on with a sharp bread knife, and his obscuring headgear removed, he went to bed and slept until the morning was well advanced. The destruction of Boyle's Farm, and the death of its owner, had done nothing to clear up the mystery that had brought him to Shepton Magna. That still remained to be solved, and, if his theory was right, very little could be done to hurry matters. It was just a question of being patient and waiting for developments.

He had told Colonel Wrayford of the scene he had witnessed in the barn, and that astonished man had agreed to follow the matter up, though it was unlikely that after the death of the principal person concerned there would be any more devil-worship in the district. Osborne had been the instigator of the whole business, in the chief constable's opinion, and, later, it was proved that he was right. Osborne had been a clergyman who had been unfrocked for some misdemeanour, and had been concerned with a similar cult in London which had been broken up by the police. Wrayford was reluctant to take any action against the people whom Osborne had persuaded to join in the orgies held in the big barn.

'There would only be a scandal,' he said. 'Much better let the thing die out. Besides, if these village people hear that there were others in with Osborne there may be a lot of trouble. I don't think it had anything to do with the murders, do you?'

Mr. Budd looked thoughtful.

'Well,' he said enigmatically, 'I do — and then again, I don't.'

During the ensuing days the big man was very busy indeed. He had taken the astonished Leek into his confidence regarding his theory, and the sergeant was given a job that kept him out for the greater part of the day. When he was sleeping, Mr. Budd took his place, and so they were never in together. This went on for nearly a week, and then one rainy evening the sergeant arrived at the inn on the bicycle that he had hired, in a great state of excitement.

'He's gone over to Loxham,' he panted.

'Right!' snapped Mr. Budd, seizing his hat. 'Come on.'

He hurried to the garage across the green, where he had already made arrangements for the use of a car, and a few seconds later he and Leek were speeding in the direction of Loxham.

'He drove to a wood near the village,' said the sergeant, 'an' there he stopped.'

'Tell me when we get near it,' grunted Mr. Budd. 'I don't want him to spot us. He'll stop in the wood until it's dark, I expect. He won't try anything until after nightfall.'

'P'r'aps he won't try anything at all; you may be wrong,' said the sergeant, and Mr. Budd snorted.

'I'm never wrong,' he retorted extravagantly, 'you'll see.'

Near the wood he stopped the car, ran it under cover of some thick bushes, and continued on foot. Presently, under Leek's guidance, he saw a car drawn up among the trees, and a man sitting on the running-board. He was reading a paper, and Leek gave a gasp.

'That ain't 'im,' he whispered. 'That feller's got a beard.'

'So he's even thought of that!' muttered the big man admiringly. 'Well, I s'pose I ought to have expected it. Now then, we'd better make ourselves comfortable. We may have a long wait.'

His words were prophetic. Darkness

229

came down, and the bearded man still sat on. He had put aside his paper, and was smoking. It was not until long after midnight that he made a move, and then quite suddenly he got up, stretched himself, and started to walk towards the fringe of the wood.

Mr. Budd followed warily. The bearded man climbed a stile and struck off across a ploughed field. After a moment's hesitation, Mr. Budd, with Leek at his heels, crept along in his wake, taking advantage of the cover offered by a straggling hedge. It meant a slight detour; but it was safer than risking the open path. Their quarry passed through a gate into a road and presently paused at the entrance to a drive that evidently led up to a large house that was invisible behind a screen of trees.

Mr. Budd gave a sigh of relief. Up to now he had been working entirely on a supposition. In order to justify his theory the bearded man had to come to this place, and the clue on which he'd built up his edifice of conjecture had been so small that, although he was certain in his own mind that he was right, this confirmation was very welcome.

The man with the beard slipped into the dark entry and disappeared. After giving him a second or two to get some little way up the drive, the stout superintendent followed suit more cautiously. He could hear the faint crunch of feet on the gravel ahead, and this gave him the approximate position of the quarry. He and Leek kept to the grass edging, and moved without a sound. Presently the tunnel of trees came to an end, and they were able to see the house. It was a large mansion, looming dimly against the night sky, and the man they were following made his way round to the back.

Watching from the shadow of a thick hedge they saw him stop beneath a small window, take something from his pocket, and fumble at the sash. There came the faintest of faint creaks, and the window was pushed up. The bearded man climbed over the sill and vanished inside the house, leaving the window open behind him.

'Come along,' whispered Mr. Budd softly, 'this is where we move quickly.'

He crept across to the window and carefully hoisted himself on to the sill. Dropping down gently on the inside he gave a hand to Leek, and the sergeant quickly joined him. There was no sound within the house, and after listening intently for a minute or so the big man took out a torch and sprayed the light round him.

They were in a small room that appeared to be a storeroom, for the walls were covered with shelves laden with jars and tins and packages. There was a door facing the window that stood ajar, and when he peered out Mr. Budd saw that there was a passage beyond. There was no sign of the bearded man, and no sound anywhere, and leaving the storeroom they made their way along to the hall. A wide staircase led upwards into darkness, and from somewhere above came the sound of a clicking lock.

Mr. Budd went quickly up the thickly carpeted stairs, moving with remarkable speed for so large a man. He came to a broad landing with a big window, and the arched entrance to a corridor. Tiptoeing down this he listened at the various doors that opened off it, and at last paused outside one halfway down on the right-hand side.

'He's in there,' he said, speaking with his lips close to Leeks' ear.

The sergeant nodded. He could hear the faint sounds from the other side of the closed door, which had told Mr. Budd into which room the bearded man had gone.

The stout superintendent waited, his ear pressed close to the keyhole. And he waited for some time. To the expectant Leek it seemed like years before, with a sudden movement, his superior flung the door open and directed the bright ray from his torch on the man who was bending over the bed.

'I want you!' snapped Mr. Budd sternly; and the bearded figure straightened with an oath. 'I want you on a charge of wilfully murdering Dr. Hickthorne, Thomas Hardiman, and George Pilcher, and of attempting to murder your

233

aunt, Miss Elizabeth Bishop, an' I warn you that anything you may say may be taken down an' used in evidence.'

The bearded man's lips curled back in a snarl.

'How did you know?' he muttered, and his hand went to his pocket.

'Keep your hand away from that revolver, or whatever it is!' said Mr. Budd sharply. 'I've got a gun, an' if you try anythin' funny I shall shoot!' He made a menacing motion with the automatic in his hand. 'Put the bracelets on him, Leek!'

The sergeant obeyed, and Mr. Budd lowered his weapon. Going over to the bed, he looked down at the grey-haired woman who lay there, her terrified eyes staring above the gag in her mouth. Her feet and ankles were bare, and round each ankle had been tied a length of stout rope.

'Go an' wake the servants!' he ordered turning to Leek. 'This lady ought to have attention.'

'What was he going to do with her?' asked the sergeant, looking with a puzzled frown at the ropes.

'Don't ask questions!' snarled Mr. Budd. 'Do as you're told!'

The sergeant departed hastily, and the big man looked at his prisoner.

'I think you'll be better without that face-fungus,' he remarked, and, going over, tore the beard away.

Alec Kilfoyle glared up at him with hate-filled eyes.

* * *

'The first thing that put me on to Alec Kilfoyle,' said Mr. Budd, in explanation to the chief constable on the following morning, 'was the ropes that we found in the old sloop. They'd obviously been faked. The knots were loose, an' they wouldn't have held a child for two minutes. Therefore, his story about bein' tied up for days, an' eventually getting free, was all bunk. An' if that was all bunk, the rest of it was bunk too. But there were two dead men in that old boat, an' if his story was all lies then it looked as if Kilfoyle had killed 'em. Which meant that there was no man with a beard at all, an' that he'd never been kidnapped like 'e said.

'I was pretty certain then that Kilfoyle was the feller we were after, but I couldn't see what his motive was. The ropes wouldn't be any good as evidence alone, an' before I could move against him I had to have somethin' more substantial. I got in touch with the Yard an' asked them to find out all they could about Kilfoyle. They discovered quite a lot, an' it wasn't to his advantage, neither.

'He'd lived in London for a time, an' got mixed up with a smart lot — night clubs an' racin' an' whatnot — an' run through no end of money. There was a firm of moneylenders from whom he'd borrowed £20,000, an' he'd done that on the guarantee of his aunt, Miss Bishop. The only trouble was that she knew nothing about it. The signature to the guarantee was a forgery!

'This firm had discovered this, and threatened to take criminal proceedings unless the debt was immediately repaid, plus the interest. Kilfoyle was in a panic.

He knew that it meant a long term of imprisonment if 'e couldn't raise somethin' like £30,000 within the three months they'd given 'im. It was no good goin' to his aunt — she didn't like 'im — an' his father hadn't got the money if he would have lent it to him.

'It was then, so he has confessed, that he thought of a brilliant idea. His aunt was a very rich woman, but she had left all her money to an old friend of her schooldays. She had told him this once, so he knew that there was nothin' doin' there. But if a later will was made leavin' her money to him, an' then she died, 'e'd be out of his trouble. The whole thing would have to be done very cleverly, otherwise the moneylenders would be suspicious. He'd have to kill his aunt without it lookin' like murder.

'Once I'd established him as the murderer of the others, it seemed obvious that he must have designs on the aunt, for she was his only hope of gettin' money. And it struck me that if he had forged a guarantee an' got away with it, he might try his hand at forgin' a will.

'He went to Dr. Hickthorne an' told 'im that 'e was writin' a book, an' he wanted to know how an elderly woman could be murdered so as it would look like natural death. The doctor told him that there was one way it could be done without poison, which was one of the things Kilfoyle stipulated. He said that if an elderly person was suspended upside down a blood vessel would break on the brain, an' the death would look like a stroke if the person was put back into a normal position after, of course.

'This was what Kilfoyle wanted, and he decided to use this means to kill his aunt an' secure the money. But Hickthorne would have to be got rid of, too, otherwise he would smell a rat when the old lady was found dead in her bed from a stroke. He thought out the plan that he eventually carried out. He forged the will an' got Hardiman an' Pilcher to witness it, tellin' 'em some story that they would swallow without question, an' then he set out to cover his tracks. The three of 'em had to be killed to avoid all trouble after the death of his aunt, an' he adopted the plan which you know. It was a stroke of genius to disappear himself, only he made the mistake of not payin' enough attention to detail.' The big man paused and yawned wearily, 'I wanted to catch 'im red-handed,' he went on, 'an' I did. I'd bin watchin' 'im fer days, waitin' for 'im to make the attempt on 'is aunt's life! I knew 'e had to do it soon because of the time limit.'

'How did you know anything about the time limit?' asked Colonel Wrayford. Mr. Budd smiled.

'That firm of moneylenders is pretty hot,' he said. 'When we knew he'd been dealin' with them it was easy. They like to keep friendly with the Yard, an' they opened their mouths wide when Inspector Dickson visited them for a little information about a client. I'm glad we got that feller,' he added — 'very glad indeed. He's a nasty bit of work.'

'But how did Osborne's devil-worshipping cult come into all this?' asked the chief constable. 'You suggested it might be connected in some way.'

Mr. Budd shrugged his shoulders.

'Kilfoyle only used it as a cover,' he said. 'He knew what was goin' on from his cousin and Miss Linley, and before committing his crimes he surreptitiously encouraged the Black Magic superstition among the villagers so that they would immediately blame the disappearances on to Osborne — human sacrifice, an' all that sort of nonsense. I'll bet, though, that even he didn't expect the villagers to go as far as they did.' He sighed. 'Well, there'll be no more of that devil-worship stuff around this part of the country, I'll warrant. Will you have a cigar, sir?'

But the chief constable, who had smelt Mr. Budd's cigars, suddenly discovered that he had an appointment.

'I thought that would get rid of him,' remarked the big man, complacently to Sergeant Leek. 'I've known the most hardened criminal wilt when I put on one o' these.'

THE END